TO Simon

Let the Blood Run Cold

With all my love

Emily Winlow

xxx

Young**Writers**

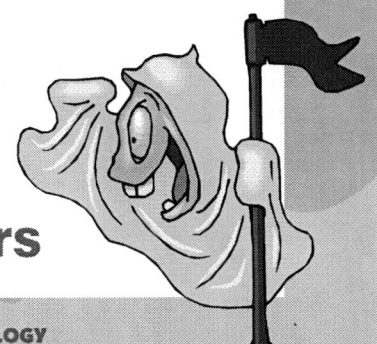

A YOUNG WRITERS ANTHOLOGY

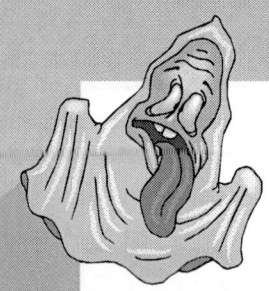

First published in Great Britain in 2004 by
YOUNG WRITERS
Remus House,
Coltsfoot Drive,
Peterborough, PE2 9JX
Telephone (01733) 890066

All Rights Reserved

Copyright Contributors 2004

SB ISBN 1 84460 591 4

Foreword

Young Writers was established in 1991 with the aim to promote creative writing in children, to make reading and writing more fun. This year we received many ghost stories from our young writers of today and within these chilling pages we have brought you a selection of the very best.

The entries we have selected highlight the children's keen interest and enthusiasm for the creation of the short story and are a showcase of the writing talents of the future. Together they will chill your imagination with their frightful and often funny tales of the supernatural.

Read on for an irresistibly hair-raising experience that will keep you creeping back for more.

A YOUNG WRITERS ANTHOLOGY

Seeing Things You Don't Want To See
Sam Mustafa (13) 12
   Death Dealer *Adam Gibson (12)* 14
   The Visitor *Samantha O'Toole (13)* 16
   Murder At The Manor *Jack Wright (13)* 18
   Spooky School *Gemma Nolan (11)* 19
   The Bone-Yard Rap *Natasha Wightman (8)* . 19
Was He There? *Amy Wiggins (11)* 20
The Reflection *Denise Paik (14)* 21
Do Ghosts Get Insomnia? *Mark Malik (12)* 22
The Warehouse Of Horror *Brandon Croft (9)* 23
The Final Cut! *Rebecca Woolcock (12)* 24
At The Top Of The Stairs *Robert Eccles (11)* 25
The Strange Hole *Aaron Turner (8)* 26
Ghostly World War II *Sidi Bai (10)* 28
The Day Of The Dead *Theodore Perehinec (8)* 28
Julie *Claire Owen (15)* 29
The Ghost In The Night *Fatima Adalbaeva (14)* 30
Murder Is Just The Beginning *Belinda Forde (13)* 32
The Dead Girl *Kamal Bhana (15)* 33
Vampire Brother *Paula Muir (12)* 34
Creak *Kathryn Brooks (13)* 35
  It Came From The Attic *Ashleigh Bayton (12)* 36
    Malicious Memory *Heidi Jones (13)* 37
     Dischord *Jessica Robb (15)* 38
     The Ghost Catcher *Jennine Bell (11)* 39
     My Lost Twin *Sethmi Pathirana (11)* 40
    The House *Joanne Mcentee (15)* 41
   A Shocking Night *Charlotte Glaves (8)* 42

Pepper *Sophie Kelly (13)*	43
Spooky House *Gemma Macdonald (10)*	44
Revenge! *Amy Boyington (15)*	45
The Boy That Never Woke Up Alive	
Rachel Stewart (14)	46
Sophie's Attic *Sarah King-Evans (12)*	47
The Haunted House *Sam Mountford (9)*	49
The Ghost Of Doom *Mike Cookson (10)*	50
Maniac Woods *Helen Griffiths (19)*	51
As I See Me *Sarah Jenkins (13)*	52
Ghost Story *Samantha Fleetwood*	53
The Tarantulas' Den *Stephanie Rainford (12)*	53
Girl On The Cliff *Charlotte Genery (12)*	54
Weird *Caroline Rainford (12)*	55
What's Your Favourite Scary Movie?	
Megan O'Rourke (12)	56
Footsteps *Adam Murphy (11)*	57
Frozen Dead *Laura Bradbury (12)*	58
How To Raise The Dead *Katie Massey (11)*	59
The House *Serina Sidhu (9)*	60
The Blacksmith And The Ghost	
Charlotte Cooper (11)	61
Death With A Vengeance *Kainaz Karkaria (14)*	62
The School Ground Ghost *Jacob Matthews (11)*	63
Lunar Relations *Emma Baillie (13)*	64
The Worst Nightmare *Joseph Mullen (13)*	67
The Magical Lake *David James*	68
The Man Werewolf *Kevin Beurskens*	69
The Chanting *Fiona Finlay (12)*	70

A YOUNG WRITERS ANTHOLOGY

Locked In (While Skipping School)
Daniel Wieringa (13) 71
   The Ghostly Room *Amy Simpson (13)* ... 72
   The Wrong Place At The Wrong Time
Alex Stephenson (13) 73
Ghost Story
   Amber Heath (12) & Kirsty Baston (10) 75
In The Barn *Nadine Rudd (13)* 76
Just Another Piano Practice *Kerry Nesbitt (13)* 77
The Prisoner Of Alamar *Maria Goodhew (13)* 78
Will You Scream? *Scott Bacon (11)* 79
Ghost Story *Lee Allen (12)* 80
Carnival Spectacular *Georgina Ann Evans (13)* 81
The Strange But Posh House *Naomi Payne (11)* 83
Gory Mansion *Jasmin Turner (11)* 84
Third Floor Bathroom *Alex Knight (11)* 85
The Man On The Ground Floor
Nicole Atkinson (12) 86
Keera's Spooky Kitchen *Craig Lyons (12)* 87
The Haunted House *Emma Steele (11)* 88
Help! *James Lees (13)* 89
I'll Be Back . . . For You! *Sophie Moran (12)* 90
   Her! *Lisa Hine (12)* 91
     The Fictional Painting *Daniel Shore (12)* 92
     Can't Escape *Nathan Monks (13)* 93
     The Girl In The Attic *Charlotte Cotterill (13)* .. 93
     Tuppences *Ellie Carding (13)* 94
     Trapped *Sarah Woods (13)* 96
     Truth Or Dare *Dan Byron (13)* 97

The Greed Within Emma Wong (14)	98
The Ghost Of Floral Cottage Bryony Willis (12)	99
Victim Amber Curtis (14)	100
The Ghost Frog Amy Mason (9)	101
The Friendly Ghosts Melissa Kelly (8)	102
Lost Charlotte Ditch (9)	103
The Unexpected Mystery Emma Wilson (8)	105
The Haunted Castle Samantha Hardy (8)	106
The Red Doll Ellen Lily Colling (9)	107
The Wicked Doll Joe Hall (8)	108
The Haunted House Jack Cessford (9)	109
The Strange Ghost Jonny Wilson (9)	110
The Ghost Wash Jessica Rump (9)	111
Haunted House Thomas Dingwall (9)	112
The Olympic Games Iona Broomes (8)	113
The Haunted House Hannah Bilton (9)	114
The Haunted Castle Helen Burns (9)	115
There's Something In The Basement *Emily Winlow (8)*	116
The Jellyfish Beach Ghost Luiza Deaconescu (12)	117
The Broomly Ghost Fay Stafford (12)	118
Victorian Ghost Emily Burnett	119
Who Is It? Nichola Mason (12)	120
The Note Abigail Bowmaker (12)	121
Adventure Accident Emma Winter (12)	122
A Walk To Remember Paul Rooney (13)	123
Silence Isra Gabal (13)	124
Flash/Bang Bethany Hammonds (13)	125
Eleven-Foot Door Andrew McCarrick (13)	126

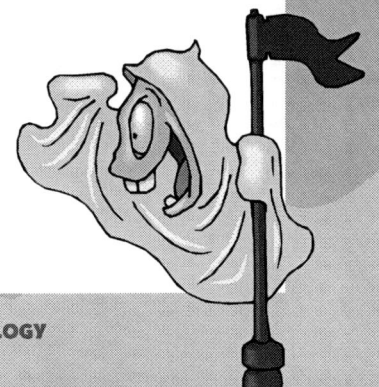

A YOUNG WRITERS ANTHOLOGY

Hallowe'en Horror *Laurie Slesser (13)* 127
The Voices *Daniella Dunning (13)* 128
The Curse Of 666
Thomas Williamson (12) 129
Face Your Fear! *Alicia McCluckie (12)* ... 130
Gory Story *Josh Palmer (13)* 131
The Night On Christmas Day
Amanda Currey (12) 132
Scream *Charlotte Lynch* 133
Haunting Elizabeth *Lauren Henden (13)* 134
Insomnia Kills *Shazia Hussain (14)* 135
Boy From Beyond *Kerry Brown (12)* 136
It's All Just Black And White
Anthony Williams (14) 137
Exorcism *Simon Jeffries (16)* 138
The Gomms *Samantha Gibbons (13)* 139
Spook Town Graveyard *Sean Jones (12)* 140
Horror House! *Keeley Knight (12)* 141
The Haunted House *Grace Taylor (12)* 142
97 Holly Street *Peter Harrington (11)* 149
The Secret Of Downs Church *Jamie Eve (14)* 150
Drip, Drip, Drip *Lily Kim-Sing (11)* 151
Eyes On A Spring *Laura Stainton (11)* 153
The Day Of Fear *Rosie Ives (11)* 154
Zombie Fright *Senem Aysan (13)* 155
Marbles *Josh Logan (12)* 157
Cannibal Parents *Hannah Redman (12)* 160
Saturday Night At The Graveyard
Catherine Smith (12) 161

A Ghastly Tale Of Ghoulish Terror
Ruth Morris (17) 162
Hallucinations *Nina Klair (14)* 163
My Ghost Story *Carrieann Machin (11)* 164
Pomponi Does Poe *Yasmin Pomponi (13)* 165
The Haunted Mansion *Faiza Hussain (12)* 166
Should Have Said No! *Sarah Tapsell (13)* 167
The Bedroom Ghost *Moa Karlin Josefsson (9)* 169
Ghost House *Paige Burnham (8)* 170

Manning Comprehensive School, Nottingham

Winter Woods *Jennifer Langton-Goh (11)* 171
The Canal's Secret *Alice Logan (12)* 172
Ghostly Melissa *Chenel Poyzer (12)* 173
The Haunted Basement *Sidra Jamil (11)* 174
Brother *Tammy Sills (12)* 175
Horror House *Amy Donnelly (12)* 176
More Than Just A Trip *Jessica Shilton (12)* 177
The Abandoned Forest *Adeeka Najabat (11)* 178
The Ghost Of Emily *Syabilla Wan Saadan (13)* 179
The Big Mistake *Asma Hussain (12)* 180
One Ghostly Day *Melissa Martin (11)* 182
The Haunted Mansion *Jade McQueen (12)* 183
The Mystery Glow *Melike Louise Berker (11)* 184
The Nightmare *Aram Mahfooz (13)* 185

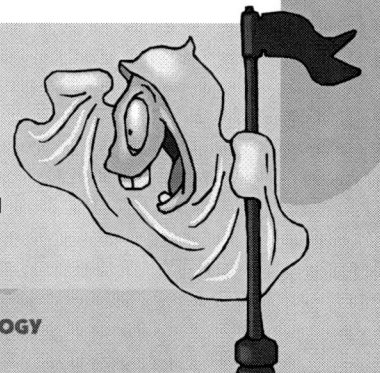

Disclaimer

Young Writers has maintained every effort to publish stories that will not cause offence.

Any stories, events or activities relating to individuals should be read as fictional pieces and not construed as real-life character portrayal.

A YOUNG WRITERS ANTHOLOGY

The Ghost Stories

A YOUNG WRITERS ANTHOLOGY

Seeing Things You Don't Want To See

The blue aura of gloom drew over the land and night filtered in. The darkness was heavy and hungry. The impending black swooped onto the streets and candlelight could not save them. It was eerie on the moor as light died. Sounds without faces lurked in the trees. Images skidded past. Noises of creatures in the night bellowed. No one could see them. Something was approaching. A looming figure of Lucifer slid along the field bringing screams with it. As it got closer, the screams got closer. It showed no sign of being human apart from a purple, bony hand outstretched from its charcoal cloak.

Only a few feet away now, a face started to appear. A pointed chin, a sinister smile and a broken, half-eaten nose. It was the eyes that scared me most. The eyes were bulging. The skin was missing around them. The whole eyeball could be seen. They were bright crimson with blood. They had been half-consumed and half left to rot.

These eyes provided light. And never in my whole life had I been so horrified of the light. Suddenly the creature vanished. A flash of white light returned to the moor.

To this day I hate light and I hate my eyes. Both of those things give the human the power to see. I know now that what I saw that evening was the reflection of my face. It was after I found I hated my eyes and etched them from my face.

Sam Mustafa (13)

Congratulations Sam! Your story wins you a fantastic family ticket to the **York, London**, or **Edinburgh Dungeons**.

A YOUNG WRITERS ANTHOLOGY

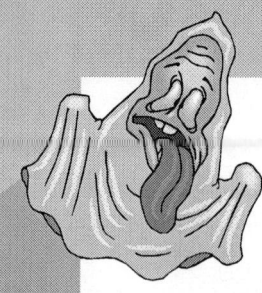

Death Dealer

This is my story of what happened when I was just five years old. It was to change my life forever.

It all started when I was on my way to market. It was 1500; a war had been raging on between vampires and werewolves. I was just five when I was savaged by a vampire and turned into one myself.

When it was dark I was able to travel. I was a death dealer from an ancient band of vampires born to hunt werewolves. My reason for killing werewolves was because if I killed as many as I could . . . well maybe I could kill the werewolf who killed my family. My hunt for the scum that did this was still on but I came closer every day.

It was five o'clock and all I could do was wait for him to return to the den. I was tracking the werewolf that I believed was Kamoon, an ancient werewolf, old enough to have killed my family. He had stopped and I began to worry that the sun may come up and I would have to stop my pursuit.

Suddenly he had came to a fast stop as he smelled me. I dropped to the ground off the high church rooftop. By the way I was now 235 years old and I knew the way to hunt by heart. The humans had become more upgraded and we had too, we had guns and silver bullets to slow those evil beasts down.

I had found the base of the howling dogs of the underworld. I had waited for this moment for 223 years. It was time to kill the blood master, the king of werewolves. I entered the den, drew my gun - liquid silver - and it was fully loaded. Suddenly two werewolves swept at me. I jumped to the roof and I blasted them. There was no coming back for them.

After killing about twenty of them, I finally came to him, the highest one of them, Kamoon. In a second I took him down. I was about to finish him.

He said, 'Why must you hunt us? The person that killed your family wasn't me.'

I said, 'Shut up, you scum of the Earth. You kill people every day and every night.'

He said, 'It was the High King Sokomo, the king of the vampires. He was the person who raised me.'

The day arrived when I was ready to kill him. At the vampire ball he proposed a speech so I grabbed an ornamental sword and I killed him and after that I ended my life . . .

Adam Gibson (12)

Well done Adam! You win a superb reading and writing goodie bag which includes a selection of books and a **Staedtler Writing Set**.

A YOUNG WRITERS ANTHOLOGY

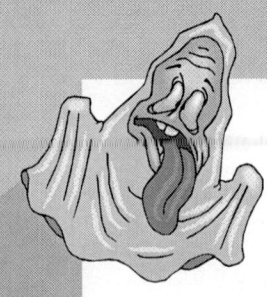

The Visitor

'At last,' said Matty as he stepped out of the gloomy graveyard. The mist hung about his body like a velvet robe as he wandered along the path towards home.

Silence was all around him, but he was used to this. The only light came from a cottage window belonging to the cemetery gatekeeper. Part of him didn't want to leave the peace of his surroundings, but thoughts of his mother pulled him along. He didn't want to be seen because nine-year-old boys should not be out at this time of night. It was different for Matty though.

Matty moved quickly, the wind blew through every part of his being. Matty remembered his mother when she used to read him stories at night, snuggled up on the sofa with a cup of hot chocolate. How he missed her.

Matty could see home. He wasn't far now. As he walked up the garden path, his heart sank. He went through the door and into the living room. He sat next to his mother. His mother was very surprised. He told his mother it wasn't her fault about the accident. Matty said, 'Stop crying Mother.' With those words his mother stopped crying and with that he disappeared.

He was so pleased he had sorted things out. As he walked back to his grave he felt sad. When he arrived back at his grave he went to sleep, never to walk again.

Samantha O'Toole (13)

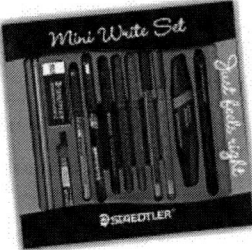

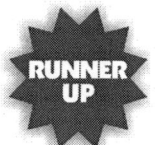

Congratulations Samantha! You win a superb reading and writing goodie bag which includes a selection of books and a **Staedtler Writing Set**. Well done!

RUNNER UP

STAEDTLER®

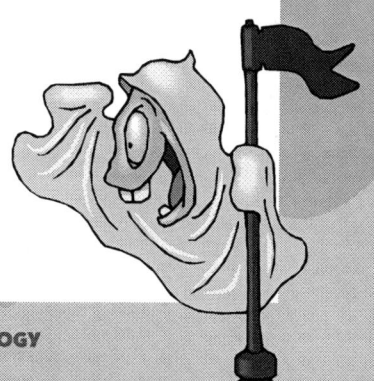

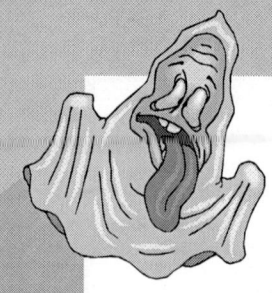

Murder At The Manor

Hi, my name's Lloyd Summers and I'm presently investigating the death of Count Seymour at his manor Misstlefoor. It all began at the grand ball.

Seymour scurried along the grand hall. He froze, a shriek came from upstairs. He rushed up and was looking around carefully. He knelt down to pick up a shiny object, the next thing that happened was there were two parts of him - body and head.

It was my turn to investigate the murder. I entered cautiously and would jump at the sound of a creak. I made my way to the crime scene. I looked, then spotted it, a tiny gap no bigger than one centimetre. I pulled the wall, revealing a dimly lit room with Count Seymour's body hanging from the ceiling with blood dripping from it. I walked back bumping into the maid, she then bid me farewell and told me return to the grand party.

I arrived at the party looking for any clues. I was watching the maid very carefully. She led a strange-looking man into the next room. I carefully followed, she locked the door behind her. I went down the hallway to find the secret door, it was behind a painting. I ripped it off and peered through the gap. She stabbed the man twice, he slumped to the floor. Lloyd was still watching when an axe hit him. He died at that spot by the person with the axe and the person that killed him was Count Seymour himself.

Jack Wright (13)

Spooky School

It was a dark and gloomy night and Sarah had returned to school to look for her book bag. She went into the classroom, when all of a sudden the lights flickered and went off, the shutters came down too. Sarah was panicking; the classroom door slammed shut. Sarah jumped and quickly hid under the desk scared half to death.

Everywhere was quiet for a while, when a cold breeze came across the room. All the hairs on Sarah's back stood on end and her teeth started chattering. She could hear footsteps moving around and voices muttering in the corridor outside the classroom. Sarah became even more frightened and she began to cry. The footsteps were getting nearer and nearer, the voices were getting louder and Sarah was crying even more. The door handle forcefully opened and footsteps came into the room. A groaning voice muttered, *'Sarah, Sarah.'*

A cold hand touched Sarah's shoulder. She woke up startled when she saw her mum sitting on the end of her bed, she realised it had been a bad dream.

Gemma Nolan (11)

The Bone-Yard Rap

100 years and 5 months ago there was a street called St Brutes and in St Brutes there was a church named St Brutes' churchyard. Every night the skeletons had a party. Every single one came to life and they danced and played all night. Nobody knew what happened there.

One spooky night in July something extraordinary happened. Would you like me to tell you? Yes or no? Yes, ok then . . .

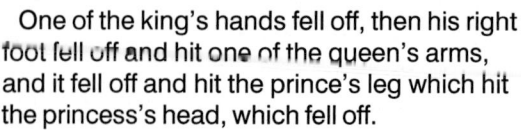

One of the king's hands fell off, then his right foot fell off and hit one of the queen's arms, and it fell off and hit the prince's leg which hit the princess's head, which fell off.

So then the skeletons played football with the head until the sun rose and the moon sank. Then all the skeletons went back to their graves and all that was left out was the princess's head which slowly dissolved into ashes.

Natasha Wightman (8)

Was He There?

Once, a long time ago, I had an experience that contained many feelings. Some scary, some, well you will need to read on to find out what these feelings were for your own thoughts. Here is my story.

In the times of no fun, I was thought to be a girl that didn't mix with others, until one day I was on my swing on my own when something caught my eye by the tree. It was tall and it looked like a boy, so I ran after *it* or him. But as I got closer to it, it seemed to sort of fade away. I stopped at the tree where it had been seen, there was nothing there to show anyone had been there and I started to think, *was it there in the first place?* That moment stuck in my head for hours.

I woke up the next morning to see it, the boy again, in my room. He did not know I was awake so I grabbed my camera and took a photo of him, the flash made him jump and turn around to face me. He looked handsome with blue eyes like the sea. He bowed and disappeared from my sight. I found myself gawking so I closed my mouth quickly.

Many days later I had my pictures back and I hurried to my bedroom. Instead of a boy, I saw nothing. So it's up to you if you believe me.

Amy Wiggins (11)

The Reflection

It was a long corridor. I was running towards the dazzling light. At the end of it there was a mirror. I looked at myself in it. But I was not there. *She* was.

I woke up sweating. I had had that dream all the time, over a whole week. I needed to do something about it. Maybe, I had to decipher the message of the dream.

I went to school, tried to concentrate in my history class and forgot about the dream. The teacher was showing some pictures as my heavy eyelids closed and finally I fell asleep.

The same corridor, the same mirror, but it was different this time. *She* was not exactly there. Instead, it was my reflection with *her* head on my hands. The bell rang. I woke up and tried to make a drawing of how *she* looked. When I finished, I realised I knew her from somewhere.

I went straight back home and had my cup of tea while reading the newspaper. When I saw the first page the cup slipped out of my hands and fell to the floor. I was shocked. It read: 'Mysterious death of a girl. She was decapitated and her head is still not found. There is no clue about the killer. A drawing of a girl's face was found near the corpse'. I looked in my folder for the drawing I had done about *her*. It was not there. I opened my

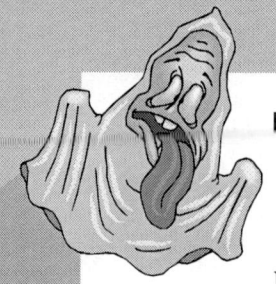

bag and didn't find the drawing, but instead was *her* head.

Denise Paik (14)

Do Ghosts Get Insomnia?

It's been a very long day; you've been to school, walked the dog, played football and done your homework. You lie down on your bed and try to get to sleep. It's been a normal day for you.

You are about to nod off, when you see some smoke. You blink and see it again. This time it completely engulfs you. You re-open your eyes and look around. Something about you feels different. You must need the toilet.

As you climb out of bed you notice that you look different. You ignore this, since you cannot put your finger on it. You walk towards the door and reach for the handle. You can't put your finger on that, either.

Instead of touching the handle, your hand goes right through it. You try again. This time, your whole body goes through it. It must've been open.

On the landing, you see a figure resembling yourself coming towards you. You think. You realise that it must be a ghost. The ghost moves towards you. Through you.

It enters your room, but it uses the door. You never closed the door behind you. It's not the ghost. *You are!*

The smoke must've killed you, but if you were dead, your living half would be dead too. Somehow, your soul left your body when you couldn't fall asleep. Your only hope is to destroy your body.

You run in front of your living self and shout, 'Boo!'

It dies instantly. But so do you!

Mark Malik (12)

The Warehouse Of Horror

One damp, dark, gloomy afternoon some boys were playing in the park, one called Ben and another called Brandon.

Ben said to Brandon, 'This is boring, let's go play inside that warehouse over there.'

'OK,' answered Brandon.

The two boys entered the warehouse carefully and cautiously. It was pitch-black inside.

'I don't think we should be in here,' whimpered Ben.

'Don't be a wimp,' answered Brandon.

'Alright but let's keep moving,' replied Ben.

Ben and Brandon's three other friends jumped out at them. 'Argh!' Ben and Brandon jumped.

'What are you doing here?' asked Brandon.

'We were looking for you,' answered Jack, one of their other friends.

'Hey lads, let's look for ghosts,' said Brandon.

'Alright,' said Jack.

The boys hunted everywhere for some ghosts, but they didn't find any.

'Hey look, there's some stairs over there,

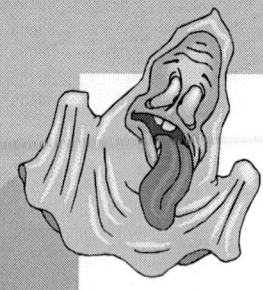

let's try up there.'

The boys ran up the stairs, there were roughly 360 steps, so the boys were tired out when they got to the top.

At the top five ghosts popped out and surrounded them, the boys were scared so they ran and the ghosts ran right after them till they got too tired to run any more. They were in a room and the door had been locked. Luckily Jack was a magician.

'Use some magic,' shouted Brandon.

'Abracadabra!' The walls were gone.

The boys ran down the stairs and out of the warehouse. They played in the park for the rest of the day.

Brandon Croft (9)

The Final Cut!

It was the first time Lilly had babysat for Jack and she was feeling nervous. He was only two years old, what if something happened? What would she do? Lilly sat down as she waved goodbye to Jack's mum. She checked on Jack who was sleeping soundly and closed the door behind her. As Lilly sat back down, she noticed Jack's mum had forgotten her mobile.

Bring, bring! The mobile began to ring and the screen read 'anonymous calling'. Jack started to cry but stopped when the phone stopped ringing. Lilly sighed with relief as she thought Jack would need attention.

The mobile rang again.

This time Lilly answered. It was voicemail. Lilly heard the sound of a baby crying. Jack began to scream, just before the mobile rang again. Lilly answered the anonymous call to hear a baby screaming. She was getting scared and it didn't help when she heard the phone ring again. This time there was a dripping sound.

Lilly went to check on Jack, but thought it was strange to see the door wide open and got extremely worried to find that Jack wasn't there. As she turned around, she saw a reflection in the bathroom mirror, little legs were hanging down. Lilly, although absolutely terrified, slowly walked into the room to be confronted by the sight of Jack hanging from a noose with a gaping cut where his tiny stomach had been, blood dripping down. As Lilly gasped the director shouted, 'Cut!'

Rebecca Woolcock (12)

At The Top Of The Stairs

It was midnight. Nothing stirred. The huge mansion loomed up, silhouetted against the night sky, deeply cast in shadow. Two darkly dressed figures scaled the cast iron gate and stole across the gravel drive. Keeping to the shadows they made their way to the door.

'Cor, come on or are you too scared?' teased Sam. In a flash Sam was gone and was already standing before the huge, panelled door.

Max caught up with him just as Sam reached for the brass knocker. Foolishly he swung it hard, the sound echoed like a bell from within the mansion.

'Sam! Why did you . . . ?' Max's voice trailed off.

Slowly but steadily, the door creaked open, age-old hinges coated in rust moved for

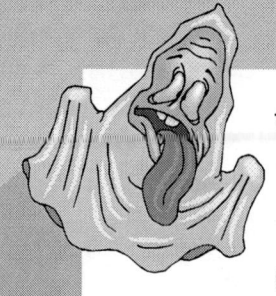

the first time in years. They stepped inside, but nobody was there. Bewildered and petrified they looked around. They were standing in a huge hall with chandeliers covered in webs and a great sweeping staircase. The whole place must have been grand, but now it was neglected.

'Wow,' gasped Sam.

Curious, he crept up the stairs but only managed halfway. For, from within the shadows floated an unorthodox, grisly form engulfed in mist. It let out a shriek and disappeared, reappearing in front of Sam. Its icy presence filled the hall. Max stood, rooted to the floor in terror. They ran, sprinting back down the staircase so fast Max didn't see Sam stumble to the ground. He flew out onto the drive and climbed the wall in haste. Turning round he realised Sam wasn't there.

Robert Eccles (11)

The Strange Hole

Lonely. She was in the woods, coming home from work. She heard a voice.

'Follow me.'

She carried on walking. Then she felt a hand on her shoulder. She panicked and ran, but she went nowhere. *What is happening? Why me?* She heard the voice again.

'Follow me.'

He dragged her away, she was scared. *Who is this man? What is he going to do to me?*

She got chucked into the back of this van and ten minutes later the doors opened. She was pushed into a house and the door was locked. It was a haunted house, she walked up the stairs to look for a way out. *Bang.* She looked up and directly in front of her was a ghost.

It said to her, *'You . . . you . . . you* have woken me!'

She said back, 'Sorry, sorry, I didn't mean to.'

It disappeared.

What was that? She saw, a hole in the wall and wondered if she could escape out of it and be set free but when she got to it she could not fit through it. She heard the voice again.

'Going somewhere?'

'No,' she replied.

She was walking backwards and didn't realise, and fell down a chute.

She landed on a pile of washing and there was a hole in the floor. She got sucked into it. It took her back home, her son was there with her husband. She shouted, 'I'm back.'

No reply.

She went to the mirror, she couldn't see herself!

Why?

Aaron Turner (8)

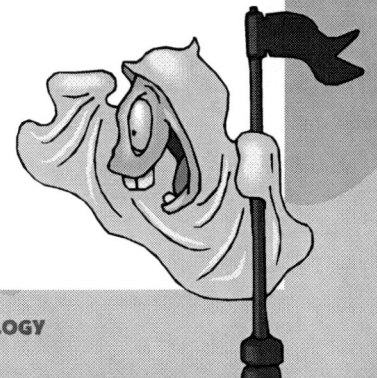

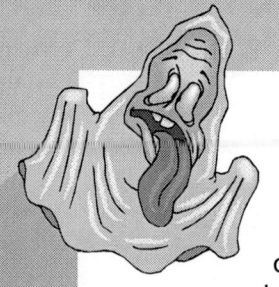

Ghostly World War II

I crouched down, hardly daring to breathe. In one hand I clutched my gas mask - in the other I felt my little brother's sweaty, trembling hand. I hugged him closer and told him not to cry. I glanced fearfully at the German planes circling above, looking for another victim spot.

A phosphorous flash brought my attention back to the forbiddingly steep sides of the dreaded trench, and as I stared at the mossy wall, a white figure in a black uniform and moustache appeared.

He bellowed at me, 'You shall die!'

I opened my mouth to scream, but it was clamped. Instead, the figure sent a thunder-roll roar of laughter echoing through the tunnels and immediately vanished. A shell came whizzing towards me and I knew no more . . .

Sidi Bai (10)

The Day Of The Dead

On the tip-tops of Symetry Mountain lived a ghost. His name was Bob. He had a box made of ribcages. Inside the box were kidneys, brains, hearts and livers that Bob had collected from the local village.

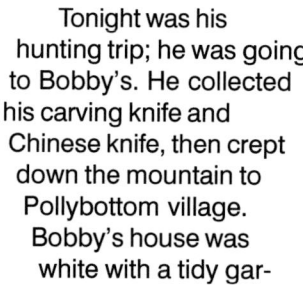

Tonight was his hunting trip; he was going to Bobby's. He collected his carving knife and Chinese knife, then crept down the mountain to Pollybottom village. Bobby's house was white with a tidy garden. He crept into the house and up to Bobby's room, then he took out his carving knife . . .

. . . He went to Sophie's house and did what he had to do. On the way home he got peckish so he nipped into McDonald's for a burger, then he went to two other houses and that was the end of his hunting trip.

Bob crept out of Pollybottom village and up to the tip-tops of Symetry Mountain and put the few organs he'd collected into the box of ribcages. Then he had tea; brain-flavoured sausages, eye jelly on toast and kidney mash potato with liver sauce all over. All his storage of organs was for the day of the dead which was on February 6th; there was only two days until the *day of the dead!*

Today was the day! They were having blood punch, intestine sandwiches and loads of other specialities. They put their collections in the box made out of ribcages . . . then all turned human for a day!

Theodore Perehinec (8)

Julie

We didn't miss her, didn't know she'd gone. Her picture was never in the yearbook, her name never on a register.

Julie, a teenage girl, sat in a geography lesson, taught by a small, old man Mr Foster.

'Can anyone tell me the capital of Kenya?' His beady eyes scanned the room, not once resting to look at Julie.

Her delicate hand was raised and she awaited upon being asked the answer.

Instead he boomed, 'Come on! We did this yesterday.' He moved forward, 'Somebody must know.'

She sat patiently, yet he never called upon her.

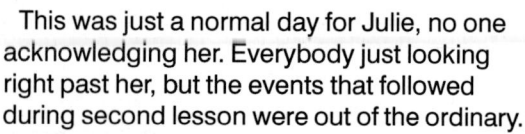

This was just a normal day for Julie, no one acknowledging her. Everybody just looking right past her, but the events that followed during second lesson were out of the ordinary.

Julie sat in maths alone, with her hand raised. She was a bright child and knew many answers others didn't. But today as the tall, slender teacher looked past her, slowly Julie's hand began to fade, becoming invisible like she had been treated for so many years.

By sixth lesson she had completely vanished from sight. Not a tear was shed by her family, not an assembly was held in her honour and not even a gravestone was given for her name.

Julie continued to attend school though, haunting the children and teachers, pulling their hair and ripping up papers, but still today no one asks where she went and no one notices her empty chair.

Claire Owen (15)

The Ghost In The Night

In life ghosts often come in different shapes and forms. They come mainly as animals like cats, goats and owls. But some can come as humans, that's what makes a ghost story more realistic, confusing and spooky . . .

Sara gingerly crept to her bedroom, hoping nobody would hear her footsteps . . .

Suddenly there was a black cat staring at her with its green, bewitching eyes. It was slowly stealthily, slinking around in the gloomy corners. It seemed to Sara that the cunning creature could read the girl's mind and knew very well, that she was afraid. Sara wanted a drink from the kitchen; there she noticed a pale face glowing in the corner.

Fearfully, she came up to the peculiar thing and shouted, 'Dad, why are you eating in the middle of the night?'

He did not answer, and continued eating his soup, making slurping, sucking sounds.

'Dad why have you painted your face? It's not Hallowe'en you know,' said Sara.

He grumbled and gave her the evil eye.

She stressed and cried, 'Fine if you don't want to answer that's fine with me.'

'Now, don't be silly Sara, your father's lying next to me, and he didn't go anywhere,' cackled her mum.

Sara then saw for herself that he was snoring beside her worse than a bear. The surprised girl ran quickly downstairs, into the kitchen and saw no sign of the ghostly figure or any trace of his food!

Back upstairs the black, mysterious cat had vanished too!

Fatima Adalbaeva (14)

Murder Is Just The Beginning

My mind was a blur wondering what was following me through this overgrown forest, knowing if I stopped it would catch up with me. I didn't know why, what or whether it would kill me.

A huge house stood in front of me.

When I got to the door I plucked up courage to see what was behind me. There was a man with a dog. They stared at me intensely, but something about the house startled the dog and he ran away yelping and the man staggered after him.

I stepped in shouting, 'Anybody here?'

No reply.

There was a screaming through the house and it felt like something touched me. I ran to the door. The door was locked.

I started rising up in the air. I tried to move, but felt totally paralysed. My body was covered with scratches. My life flashed before my eyes and I fell to the ground.

A woman was found dead at the gates of a house. Tom Hindly went in with his police dog and saw a figure running. He said it looked like the woman who was found dead. When he got to the house he saw it stand and look at him, then his police dog ran away yelping so he went to find him.

People have witnessed seeing this same figure sitting by the window and sometimes hearing it cry and calling, but no one knows what it is and no one is willing to find out.

Belinda Forde (13)

The Dead Girl

It was cold and dark and as I stepped out onto the wet pavement, I pulled my jacket tightly around myself to retain warmth. Within seconds, my hair was drenched and tousled. I began to quicken my pace.

I turned the corner and there I noticed a young girl sitting on the pavement, wrapped in a tattered brown blanket. Her arms were covered in bruises, her skin was ghostly pale and blood was dripping from her mouth, forming a dark pool of blood beside her.

I hurried over to her and attempted to make conversation. 'What's your name?' I asked her.

She just sat there rocking back and forth slightly but she did not answer.

I asked her how she had obtained the bruises on her arms - again, silence.

Suddenly she looked up at me. Her face, twisted into a malicious smile. I saw a glint in her eyes as she whispered, 'Mummy tried to kill me - I killed her!'

She then began to crawl towards me, her grin widening as she drew nearer to me. I became afraid and my instincts urged me to run, and so I did. I sprinted back to my apartment, unable to believe what I had just experienced. I turned on the television to take my mind off the horrible encounter and the face of that horrifying girl filled the screen. The headline read: 'Young girl killed mother in heated argument a week ago'. That was definitely the girl I had just seen!

Kamal Bhana (15)

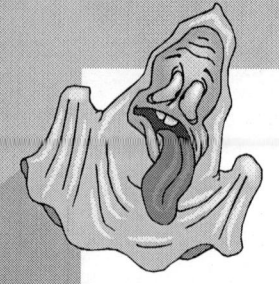

Vampire Brother

'Gotcha,' snarled Harry with his face pressed against my neck.

It was Hallowe'en and we were going trick or treating, so my 8-year-old brother, Harry, decided to go as a vampire and I, however, went as a witch. I'd never liked trick or treating, but I just went for Harry's sake.

And so we went, house after house, until our bags were full and Harry got tired.

'Michelle, I'm tired, can we go home now please?'

'Oh alright then, but next time let's not go so far because every year you always moan at me because you're bored, and as if it's my fault!'

'Mum, Mum, look how many people gave me sweets,' shouted Harry as he bombed through the door.

'Oh that's great honey,' said Mum trying to sound delighted. 'Put them on the side and go and get ready for bed.'

We both brushed our teeth and got into bed. I feel asleep, dreaming of our trick or treating night. Suddenly I heard a noise, a noise as if someone was right beside me. Then it got louder and nearer so opened my eyes and turned to my left.

'Argh!' Argh!' I screamed so loudly my mum and dad came bursting into my room.

'Harry what on earth are you doing?' my mum said, looking as shocked as I was.

My brother was leaning against my neck, two teeth about twice the size of his others. 'I need blood, soooo thirsty,' croaked Harry.

At first I thought it was a laugh. 'OK . . . ha, ha . . . very funny Harry, now go away and shut my door.' But then he gave me an odd look and I realised he wasn't joking.

'Sooo thirsssty,' Harry said again.

Paula Muir (12)

Creak

It was a dark and misty Friday night. We all dared each other to stay in the lonely, haunted house that was in the middle of the deserted field. The house had never been sold since the family that owned it just disappeared . . .

We all accepted the dare. There was Chanttell, Alison, Tina and me, Kathryn. When we got there we stepped up to the front door, but to our surprise the door flung open. We all walked in, then the door slammed shut behind us. We thought nothing of it.

We set up our sleeping bags, ready for us to sleep in and we put all our stuff away.

Alison said, 'Let's go and explore the house.'

So we did. I started to walk upstairs.

I heard Tina say, 'I think there is someone watching us. Did you hear that?'

We just laughed thinking the rumours were getting to her and she had imagined it.

As we were getting ready for bed Chanttell screamed, 'Did you see that?'

But no one else saw anything. We could hear the floorboards creak and we could see the shadows. We were scared.

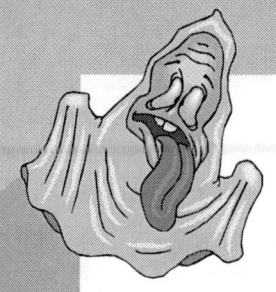

While we were in bed the windows and doors started to move, then swing. The floorboards started to creak even louder. Out of nowhere we could suddenly see the family that disappeared, reappear before our eyes.

They whispered, 'Get out, run away as fast as you can, don't come back unless you want to be like us; it's coming!'

So we ran and ran and ran and never went back.

Kathryn Brooks (13)

It Came From The Attic

'Bye Mum!' said Ella.

'Bye sweetheart, I'll be home around 9pm,' her mum said rushing out of the door.

'Yes, alone in the house,' she said excitedly. She wandered upstairs and started to watch telly.

Suddenly a loud thumping noise came from the attic. It sounded like giant footsteps. It stopped. Slowly and carefully Ella opened the door. Whilst walking carefully she listened. Again she heard the sound, but much louder and much closer. Looking around she ran downstairs and grabbed the phone. The phone lines were dead. They had been cut. Crying with fear she slowly staggered upstairs, then opened the attic door. What she saw scarred her for life.

It was a pale man with his stomach cut out. He had a distinctive smell, the smell of someone who died a long time ago.

'W-w-w-who are you and why are you here?' she cried.

'I have come for revenge. Your father did this to me.' The ghost spoke with a deep voice.

The door downstairs opened, Dad was home.

'The murderer downstairs awaits you.' The ghost was scaring Ella now.

From downstairs she heard her father calling for her.

'You choose who you believe then huh?' he mumbled.

'I'll never believe you. Dad, I'm coming,' Ella said in a put on voice.

Ella ran downstairs but tripped. She cried out for her father. He never came.

Ashleigh Bayton (12)

Malicious Memory

One in ten people begin life as a twin in the womb. An old wives' tale defines the word 'twin' as one purely evil soul and one purely good soul, it then goes on to tell us that in a large majority of cases in which one of the twins die, the surviving twin has a balance of good and evil within them.

I am a surviving twin. In my mother's womb I had to fight for nutrients against an identical sister who died after birth when her body could no longer pull through the ordeal. A replica of myself died fifteen years ago to the day. The doctor told me I was lucky to have survived, yet I don't hold the same enthusiasm. It haunts me every day, every night, every time I see that creature, seemingly innocent and vulnerable. The mere thought of it offers clammy hands, prickled skin and alarmed senses to my body. The memories came rushing back. Last time it was over I promised myself that it would never happen again, I wouldn't let it bother me but it's my shadow, stalking me. I can smell, hear and see it. But it isn't as comforting to me as it would be to you. Everything is black and white, its eyes are suspicious, its cries of laughter are filled with darkness. For my ghost is worse than anything you could ever imagine, it is the memory of my twin, who I killed fifteen years to the day.

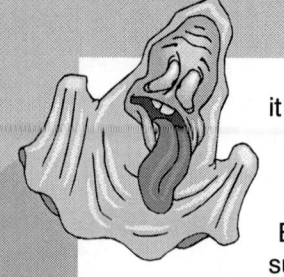

Heidi Jones (13)

Dischord

There was not a single sound except the deep rhythmical breathing of a little girl. She was surrounded by childhood dreams - teddy bears, rocking horses, inanimate and unbreathing, and a miniature piano. In the next room her parents were also asleep. The house was silent.

A solitary note rang out from the miniature piano. Then another. A failed chord, clashing. The girl stirred. She was confused. She rubbed her eyes but her vision was blurred. Something had changed. It was icy cold. She gripped her bedclothes closer around her, but as soon as she moved an animal instinct told her to freeze. She felt, more than heard, a slight movement of air, like someone was walking across the room.

She moved her mouth into the shape of a scream. The same instinct had closed up her throat. She felt compression at the end of her bed. She was being drawn towards someone sitting there. She squinted in the dark, straining to see.

But she couldn't see anything. She lay, frozen. Gradually her muscles relaxed. She didn't feel threatened. Again, her rhythmical breathing filled the room.

A watery sun seeped in and the child thought nothing of the events of the night. But as she was falling asleep the next night she dreaded those notes from the piano, solitary, then together, clashing. Quavering, the reverberations lasting into the night.

Jessica Robb (15)

The Ghost Catcher

Everyone knew about the ghost-infested castle that was until a father and daughter moved to the village. The daughter, Caroline, was extremely adventurous and really wanted to explore in the castle.

On the next Saturday her dad was away so she thought this was the perfect time to go to the castle. She walked up to the rusty, iron gates and opened them cautiously.

Caroline walked along the cobbled path up the stairs and stood in front of some towering, wooden doors. She reached up just managing the handle. The door creaked as it opened. She was about to creep in when she heard something. It whizzed quickly over her head. It was a little white ghost with a present and a tissue.

Caroline was laughing at the same time as being confused and a chill ran down her spine. She took two steps forward and the door slammed behind her. She fell forward on her face, and was about to leave when she heard a cry of laughter.

She was still confused about the ghost and present, and being adventurous as she was, she walked towards the room of laughter. The small black door was slightly open so she peeked in what could it be: a birthday, holiday or . . . In the room was a *coffin* but everyone was dressed casual and bringing presents - *weird*.

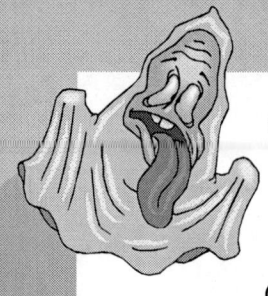

Caroline walked towards the entrance. *Creak! Creak!*

'Argh!' she screamed.

Jennine Bell (11)

My Lost Twin

Hi I'm Elisa. I live in Northernville with my parents. There's Elly too, she's my twin sister, yet I'm an only child now, I've lost her.

It started in the new house. I went to a friend's place and was dropped off late at night. The howling wind stung my eyes. I ran home, passing the three graves in front of our house, then I saw something.

'Elly, your name's on that grave!'

'Elisa come in at once,' my mum shouted.

I told her what I'd seen, but she laughed.

During the next few days strange happenings took place. When I was walking down the stairs, I met Elly. Suddenly I tripped and hurt myself. Despite being hurt I laughed and turned to look, but where was she? I couldn't see her anywhere.

'Stop playing hide-

and-seek,' I began and then answered, 'I just wanted to play you know.'

I turned to go when a voice called, 'No, I wanted to say hello. Bye.'

I ran to my room after that incident. I was called to dinner and the voice came again.

'Come, let's play.'

This time I could see her. I picked up my book and threw it at her. She started bleeding.

The door opened. My dad came in. Blood was everywhere. He looked at me. He saw nothing strange, but he seemed frightened. I slept with my parents that night. We left the next day.

Elly's dead, but her voice echoes in my head.

Sethmi Pathirana (11)

The House

'Janie.' A timid voice called out to the shadows. 'Janie, where are you?'

No reply came. Brooke took a timid step further along the darkened corridor. She knew it had been a bad idea to come here in the first place. It had been Janie's idea. Janie thought it would be a brilliant idea to sneak out of their houses and play in the house. Everyone in the village knew the terrible legend of that house and nobody dared go near it.

'Janie, this isn't funny anymore!' Brooke shouted loudly.

There came a huge crash from behind her. She spun but saw nothing. Her eyes began to well with fresh, salty tears. She carried on down the passage, her footsteps quickening; she had to get out.

A loud thud came from the wall and she jumped into the wall on the opposite side but even when she strained her eyes, she couldn't make out anything. She could now hear her heart pounding; the silence of the old mansion making it sound like the fast beat of a drum. Her whole body trembled. She spun once more and sprinted down the corridor; her eyes streaming. She was reaching the end when she heard heavy footsteps chasing her. Spinning around she saw the figure of her friend Janie.

'Janie?" Brooke called out, a little scared.

The pale figure smiled at her and then walked away, right through the wall.

Joanne Mcentee (15)

A Shocking Night

Long, long ago there was a jolly couple who lived at Greenhill Street. They were a kind family but in 1955 there was a disease, so the Greenhill family, who were thought to have fled to Japan, hid in the cellar.

They stayed there until 1967. There was no food or water down there so they perished in the cellar.

A couple of years later a family from France moved into Greenhill House.

That first night, as they snuggled down in their posh beds, something cold passed near and stared at them. It was the ghosts of the Greenhill family.

The French family were petrified by the transparent looks on the ghosts' faces. Claire, the mother ghost, said in a very threatening way, that if they ever entered the cellar they wouldn't come out. The French family were speechless.

That morning they woke with relief and went to see if the tale was true!

Charlotte Glaves (8)

Pepper

Joe Holmes felt hollow inside. He felt like a part of his heart was missing. He lay in his bed and stared at the stars. They had lost their twinkle and hung dimly in the dark sky. He couldn't get over the fact that Pepper, his bouncy Border collie was gone. He missed hearing him snuffling in his sleep, legs twitching . . .

He woke with a start, his heart pounding like a drum. He was sure he could hear a dog barking. He leapt out of bed and ran to the window. He could see a faint glimmer, but it was too dark to see anything clearly and the barking continued. Before he realised what he was doing, he was hurrying downstairs to the back door, trying to be as quiet as possible. Surely his mum and dad could hear this? He unlocked the back door silently and ran into their untidy garden.

His mouth hung open. A translucent Pepper stood waiting for him. 'Pepper,' Joe whispered. The dog launched himself at Joe and tried to give him a huge lick on the cheek. It felt like somebody had pressed an ice cube on it. It wasn't possible. Pepper was dead. But everything seemed so real, especially the icy lick on his cheek. *Even if it is a dream,* he thought, *it's still a chance to say a proper goodbye to Pepper. Tears rolled down Joe's cheeks, but as he looked up he smiled weakly. The stars were twinkling once more.*

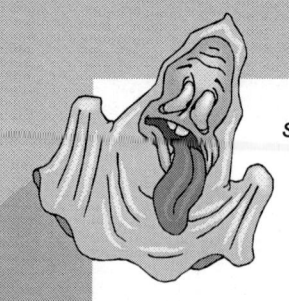

Sophie Kelly (13)

Spooky House

On a cold, wet, windy winter's night, while I was in the house on my own, sitting by a nice, big fire, the lights started to flicker. The wind was howling and I was getting very scared. I thought I heard my dog, outside the sitting room door, shaking himself from the rain as it was very wet out there, so I went to see if my mum had come in from feeding the other animals. When I opened the sitting room door to let the dog in, he was not there, so I went to check to see if he was in any other room of the house. No sign of the dog.

By this time I was even more scared. I went back into the sitting room, closed the door and sat by the fire again. Just as I had sat down to warm myself by the fire, the lights went out. I was, by this time, out of my mind with fright and I started to call out for my mum.

When she came in she said to me, 'Have you seen the dog?'

I said, 'I thought the dog was with you.'

She said, 'The dog ran away from the lightning.'

When my dad came in I said to him, 'You will have to go and look for the dog.'

So what was shaking

outside my sitting room door I never found out but it still scares me when I think about it. I'm sure my house is haunted.

Gemma Macdonald (10)

Revenge!

Suddenly, I woke up, sitting bolt upright in my bed. I strained my neck. I heard it again . . . the sinister whistling. I thought I had been dreaming it, but no, I could hear it now. Where is it coming from? I got out of bed, opened the old oak door, it creaked, my heart silently pounded. The floorboards beneath me were icy cold. I shivered. I couldn't shake off the eerie feeling, the hairs stood up on the back of my neck. I could feel another's presence.

'Hel-hello?' I said shakily. No reply. Perhaps it's my crazy imagination. Yes, that's it, I must have been dreaming, or thinking the worst as usual . . . the whistling started again. I stopped dead in my tracks, transfixed to the spot. Icy cold droplets of sweat slid down my forehead. What the hell is going on? My mind is racing, heart pounding. The whistling stops, all is silent, then all I hear is a deathly whisper.

'Help me!'

The voice sends shivers down my spine. 'Help, help who?' is all I manage to say. I stare into the darkness but see nothing.

'Me.'

Then out of the darkness all I see is a strange mist swirling in the hallway, coming straight for me. I see the outline of a delicate woman. In her hand she holds a small, wooden flute, it's pearly-white like her body. In the other she holds a dagger, which glints in the moonlight. Her expression is that of determination and sadness.

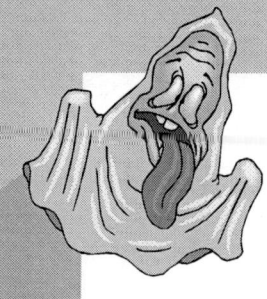

'Help me,' she whispers again, 'to get revenge on your ancestor.'

'How . . . I don't know, why? Why?' I want to go and run but I am too scared.

She looks at me and whispers, 'Your ancestor killed me, many years ago and he will pay.'

I took a look at her face, her expression was of a mad woman, her eyes bulged out of their sockets, she was shaking with fury. She raised the dagger and plunged it with all her might into my heart. As I collapsed all I heard was the triumphant shrieking of the ghost.

'I told you Master Witick that I would get my revenge, one day!'

Amy Boyington (15)

The Boy That Never Woke Up Alive

Drip, drip, drip was the sound of water or blood? Mike stopped in his tracks. He was cold and shivering. He could hear the faint cry of a little girl. He searched the darkness everywhere. His heart was thumping; somehow from nowhere the little girl was right in front of him. Mike ran after her with a pile of questions in his mind. Why was she running? Who or what was she running from? What were all those noises? Where was he? Mike finally caught up with her. As he looked around he gasped; he thought he saw a suspicious man walk past. No, it was just his imagination playing tricks on him. He was in pitch darkness and your mind does that sometimes.

'He's coming!' the girl whimpered.

'Who is?' said Mike turning towards her, his voice was trembling with fear.

As she turned round, 'Argh!'

Mike woke up gasping for air. His parents came running to his aid.

'Another nightmare?' his mother asked.

'It was real, he's coming!' exclaimed Mike.

'Sshh,' said his mother as she comforted him.

'The girl had bl . . . '

'Try to get some rest,' his mother interrupted.

That following morning Mike's body was missing. There was blood all over his room. It was all over his bed, walls - everywhere, except on one white piece of paper and on that piece of paper it said, *'I'm coming'*.

Rachel Stewart (14)

Sophie's Attic

Sophie moved into a house not long ago. Her mum and dad hated her so she had her room in the attic. Ever since she had gone into the attic she was traumatised. What that family didn't know was that the attic was haunted. Every night at midnight ghosts soared through the attic tearing everything apart.

One night a ghost flew into Sophie's body and sent an ear-piercing scream through the house. Sophie was then led into a room where she stayed until 5pm.

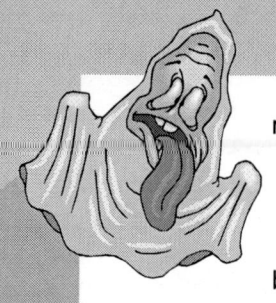

Every night she went into the room and she always came out at 5pm.

In the morning her face went paler and paler but her parents didn't care. Sophie didn't know why she was getting ill or how. Sophie only remembered a small creature. It was transparent and had no arms or legs.

It soon became bedtime and at midnight Sophie was up staring at her clock. The chimes chimed twelve times and the attic rattled.

Sophie screamed and ran for the door but it was locked. The ghosts ran for her and she couldn't get away in time. The ghosts ripped the books in half and threw them at her.

Next day Sophie woke up in hospital surrounded by police.

Sophie's parents were put in jail because it looked as if they had abused her. She wasn't sad about this because they hated her and she hated them.

Sophie was adopted and had loving parents. She never lived in an attic again.

Sarah King-Evans (12)

The Haunted House

One chilling night two friends got lost in a storm. Their names were Jonathan and Emily.

'Come on Jonathan!' shouted Emily. 'My parents are waiting in Mow Cop Mansion.'

So they ran but didn't get any closer because they were lost. After travelling for two hours they got there.

The door creaked open and cautiously in they walked. The whole house was covered in a layer of dust and cobwebs. They looked around for any sign of Emily's parents but everywhere looked dead and dusty. They saw the stairs and looked at one another to see if they dared go up. Jonathan nodded to Emily and they started to go up very carefully. The stairs creaked and shook as they walked and they were scared and shaking themselves. As soon as they got to the top they both screamed in horror as they saw a shape move towards them. As it got closer they could see it was a man in a cavalier outfit with his head tucked under his arm. There was nothing on top of his neck at all except blood and guts. They both knew it was *Baron Chop Head!*

They ran until they got outside and saw a flash of light. It was Emily's parents' car.

'Dad, get us out of here!' said Emily.

'Not without your mum,' her dad replied.

'Argh!' the kids shouted with horror.

The ghost walked up to them and it turned into Emily's mum. So they drove off laughing.

Sam Mountford (9)

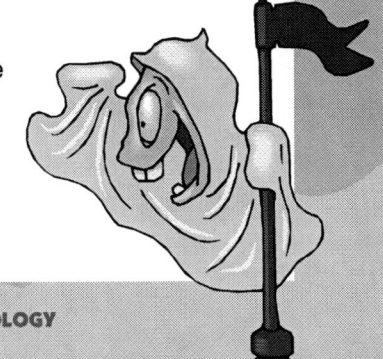

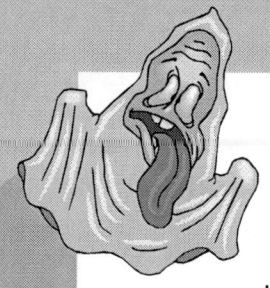

The Ghost Of Doom

One evening at about 5pm two children took their dog out for a walk. Their names were Holly and Tim. As they came to the end of the track, they stopped. The wind rustled through their hair and the leaves danced around them. All of a sudden, music appeared in their ears. It was coming from the little church across the field. Archie, the dog, started barking furiously, his hackles ran straight up.

'What is that?' said Tim.

'I don't know,' Holly whispered nervously.

'Let's check it out,' said Tim.

So they headed towards the church. They came towards an old rustic gate that led into a graveyard. They walked up the huge footsteps sheepishly. Tim knocked on the gigantic door. No answer. He tried again, this time it flew open.

Tim and Holly walked in. They saw footprints leading to a door. They followed them, through an opened door. There in front of them was this white ghostly figure coming down the stairway. The figure came closer to them as it came they could see right through the ghost and could see the stairs through it. It came closer and they could see it was a woman dressed in medieval clothes. She started to run after them. They turned around and ran out of the church closing the door behind them. The ghost ran straight through the door and passed the children and ran off into the distance, never to be seen again.

Mike Cookson (10)

Maniac Woods

It was a gloomy night as the bus load of cheerleaders were travelling to the State Cheerleading Competition. Suddenly there was a huge bang as the engine blew and the windows shattered. The cheerleaders ran into the eerie woods before the bus exploded. They all went silent when one of the girls screamed. They huddled together when they heard choking and gasping in the distance. Two of the girls had vanished, the rest tried to run but were too slow. They were scratched by twigs, tripping over roots and were panicking.

Suddenly a masked man jumped out of nowhere with a huge, rusty machete and the head of one of the cheerleaders; her face drowned in blood and fear. The man and his weapon were also covered in blood. The maniac ran towards the cheerleaders as they turned and ran for their lives. He was too quick as he glided through the woods and slaughtered them when they fell. Everything seemed to be coming to an end as the group of cheerleaders were rounded down to three. They thought they'd lost the masked maniac so they hid.

They were crying with fear when they heard heavy breathing and footsteps dragging through the leaves. The three girls thought this was it as a figure stood before them. It was another cheerleader covered in deep cuts and blood. The other three helped her as they ran towards the burning bus.

They were relieved when the police turned up to help. The tragedy was over.

Helen Griffiths (19)

A YOUNG WRITERS ANTHOLOGY

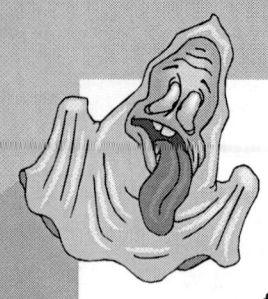

As I See Me

It started at midnight when everyone was asleep in the house but me. Something was keeping me awake. I noticed the sound. It was faint footsteps. I jumped out of bed and slowly walked onto the wooden landing. It was lit with just the light from the moon hidden behind the clouds. I decided to run down the stairs to catch them red handed.

I ran into the living room first. When I looked around the first time I didn't notice anyone there. I noticed that the trees were crashing against the window. I thought that was what I'd heard. I then looked into the mirror that was above the dark, open fireplace which had the logs piled neatly by. I spotted a tall figure standing in the corner of the room with a hood over its head so I couldn't see who it was. I screamed. The voice said there was no point. I asked why. The voice told me to look into the mirror again. When I looked into it I couldn't see my body or any parts of it.

The voice said to me, 'You are now one of us where no one sees you.'

I then realised what he was telling me. *I was a ghost.* I asked the voice why.

He answered me and said, 'You heard our faint footsteps.'

What was I going to tell Mum? That was not a worry right now. All I was concerned about was that I was a ghost.

Sarah Jenkins (13)

Ghost Story

Ali Parker had just moved into a mansion on her birthday. She loved the way it looked - old with huge trees, one at each side of the house.

Late that night she climbed into bed. As she shut her eyes Ali heard footsteps coming towards her. To her shock a snow-coloured figure stood and stared at her.

'Leave this house or else,' the ghost ordered.

Ali rushed out of bed and ran out of the room. Her head was pounding, her face was dripping with sweat. It looked as though she was melting. Ali ran down the stairs struggling to breathe. Her eyes were like waterfalls. As she arrived at her front door another ghost was blocking her way out. This time the ghost had a knife. Her throat was as dry as overcooked bread.

Then things got worse. The lights started flickering. Ali fell to the floor in fear. All of a sudden the lights stopped flickering. The ghost had disappeared. Ali stood up, then to her shock some of her family and friends jumped from behind the sofa and shouted, *'Happy birthday Ali!'*

Samantha Fleetwood

The Tarantulas' Den

Now, everyone knows that many tarantulas are extremely venomous. A family in Mexico was invaded by a massive number of 'Red Kneed' tarantulas. There were at least eight million.

At 1.15 in the morning Rosé, the 16-year-old daughter, was awakened by the dog who was barking horrifically at a 'Red Kneed' tarantula that had made its way onto the bedroom ceiling, right above her bed. Rosé closed her eyes but could not stop thinking about that big eight-legged creature resting above her.

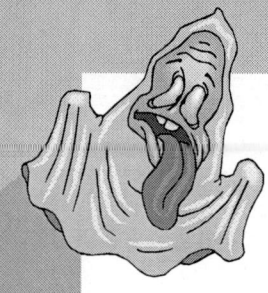

Again she opened her eyes to see the thing dangling only 30 centimetres above her nose.

The next thing she knew three more tarantulas were following the first. She noticed white marks on her walls. They were webs that led out into the hallway. Rosé followed the webs and ended up in her father's room. She realised the web was also around his walls. She ran and woke her father up and told him about the tarantulas in her room. She peered behind her because she could hear scuttling on the wooden floorboards. Rosé leapt on the bed to hug her father. They both crept to the kitchen to find not one tarantula but around eight million. Everywhere they looked were tarantulas!

Eventually, after a day or two, Rosé decided to keep them as pets!

Shocking aye!

Stephanie Rainford (12)

Girl On The Cliff

A windswept girl stood far in the distance. Nobody knew her name but just her past.

A year ago a terrible thing happened in a small village named Recconsly. Strange things were going on, weird folk turned up in cloaks cursing the elderly, taunting the young. Everyone was distraught, the more they tried to stop it the more the folk haunted. The village was going into ruins. The people were losing hope.

A leader came, he was far worse than the others. He was killing. All he did was click his fingers and they dropped dead on the spot. He shot out five-legged frogs from his fingertips, which ate all the crops.

By then there were only a few people left. He then ordered half men, half lions to go and suck up all the dead. They say they shot them in slime to make them taste better. Then the leader killed all the rest, apart from one family, he wanted to kill them differently. They were both placed on large poles with rope around their necks, they let go of the rope, the leader took down his hood which was a disgusting sight; his face was all rotten and he had no eyeballs just glowing red sockets. He shot green sparks at them.

Now the girl who had seen the occasion had managed to escape and here she is standing on the cliff . . .

Charlotte Genery (12)

Weird

I was sitting in my room daydreaming when suddenly the door opened. Someone in black was coming towards me with something dangling from his hand. The next thing I knew I was walking in total darkness, but then I fell and I could finally see again. I looked at the thing in black and he took his hood off. I screamed as loudly as I could, but no one heard me. Every second it was getting hotter and hotter.

Right in front of me was a big rock. Lava started to fill the room but I jumped onto the rock. Before it exploded the black-coated thing grabbed me and pulled me back. He led me and I was pushed in. Unexpectedly I dropped into a hole, but then I stopped and started going upwards. The walls were weird and mysterious, colourful too. In ten seconds I was standing at another door and I opened it, and found that it was my room. I then closed the door and opened it again. The red and orange colour wasn't there, but my house was. The thing that was dressed in black was a skeleton which had come up from the dead.

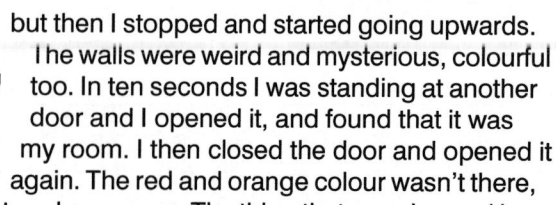

I went downstairs to find my mum, but when I did find her she had horns on her head, a big red, pointed tail on her back, and she was red all over. When I looked in the mirror, guess what . . . ?

Caroline Rainford (12)

What's Your Favourite Scary Movie?

One cold, windy night Cindy and Bobbie were in their new house watching 'Why The Devil Killed Me!' They were sitting on the edge of their seats and were really freaked out.

Cindy stared straight at the Devil, the Devil looked like it was coming out of the screen. Cindy walked to the toilet and the Devil's eyes followed her upstairs. Cindy took ages, so Bobbie went to go and get her. When they crept down the stairs the film went all fuzzy but nothing had happened or changed. They listened to a bit of music and could hear weird voices like, 'Cindy come upstairs, we're waiting and this knife is pretty sharp'.

Cindy looked up and carried on listening to music. Then a toy clown fell down the stairs.

Bobbie said to Cindy, 'I put that daft clown in the suitcase and the suitcase is locked.'

Then there was tapping on the window. Cindy went to look.

The door slammed down, this evil spirit came in. It was like the huge Devil, the same as the one on the video. It pushed Cindy on the floor and broke her legs and pulled out one of her bones. He dragged Bobbie by his hair and drowned him in the bath.

All the blood floated down the drain where the spirit had ripped open Bobbie's throat.

A couple of years later the police found the bodies and they were all rotten and smelt revolting. They had the house cleaned up and put it up for sale and guess what? No one put an offer in for it!

Megan O'Rourke (12)

Footsteps

When I came home from school I could hear my grandma's footsteps coming from the kitchen. When I came out of the bath, I heard my grandma's footsteps coming up the stairs to throw me my clothes. Whenever I shouted, she was there. I always heard my grandma's footsteps. But, one time I didn't.

It was a Saturday. I always sleep at my grandma's house on Saturday night. Strange, my birthday was the next day, I would be 6 years old. It was 9pm, I wanted to wake up early so I went to bed straight away at bedtime. At bedtime I got myself in bed and I heard my grandma's footsteps coming in. She walked into my bedroom and came over to me. She kissed me, whispered goodnight and walked out of the room and back downstairs. I fell asleep.

I woke up.

Bang! I looked over to the window. Through my curtains I could see a shadow, a shadow of a person. It was watching me. I couldn't move.

Smash! In my grandma's bedroom the window smashed and I looked up at the person.

'Grandma!' I yelled.

The person grabbed an object and hit me. That was the time I never heard my grandma's footsteps. But I always hear them now, no matter what. And the disappointing thing is, I never got to turn 6 years old . . .

Adam Murphy (11)

Frozen Dead

Thud! Thud! Thud! There was that sound again. I thought it was just in the house, but I was outside so how could it be?

I heard it again, the same sound hammering inside my head, or was it outside? I wasn't sure. I was in a state by now. I wasn't scared of the house, just the noise.

I had to find out what it was, so I went round to the back of the house.

The sight was appalling - bodies falling from trees and bushes, just left there frozen stiff, but alive.
They were all still alive.

Then suddenly the silence was broken with screams of pain and terror. I just wanted to cry and run, but I couldn't escape. I felt a force pulling me down into the mud. I tried to pull free but without success. I was now waist deep in mud. I knew I would not last much longer. I knew that I could not hold on. I knew it was the end.

Laura Bradbury (12)

How To Raise The Dead

Usually books are useful and help you, but I never expected to pick out a book that would change my life forever.

'Now, you need the library for this research. We are looking at ancient Egyptian mummies and kings,' explained my boring history teacher.

Great, a boring trip to the boring library for boring research, this is definitely going to be the most enlightening trip ever. *Not!* But if only I knew it would be a little too enlightening for me, or anyone to handle.

The weather was nice and hot. I felt annoyed that I had to do research. I set my books out on the table and walked over to the history section.

'Ow!' A book had fallen on my foot. I bent down to see what it was. 'Forbidden Magic,' I read out loudly. The lights went out and suddenly I was alone. 'Uh-oh. I need something to bring them back.' I said aloud the next paragraph of spells. 'Parlumas Comprendai!' I was at a graveyard. And it was no longer daylight. I felt scared. Should I risk another spell? I flicked through the book. 'Dereechay un uradeed!' Nothing happened. I spun around. A decayed hand was poking out of the soil. I stared, mouth open. It moved. I backed up and tripped over. Zombies surrounded me,

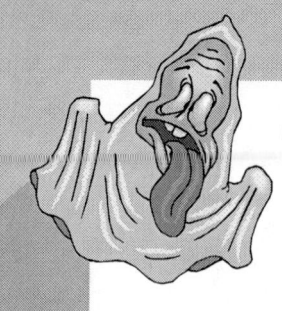

moaning and groaning, their bony, decayed hands grabbed at me.

'Atrono reverso.'

They disappeared and I was back in the library, or was I . . . ?

Katie Massey (11)

The House

There was a dark, gloomy house on a corner of a street with no lights and no sign of life, except for one sign of life that was shadows. The house was so gloomy people never ever went near it. They said it was haunted, but there was one girl in the village who was braver than all the other villagers.

'I'm going to prove that the place is not haunted,' she said one morning while walking away.

She wasn't seen for two days. However when she did turn up she looked as white as a sheet.

'What's wrong me girl?' asked the girl's dad, in a Scottish voice. 'Well?'

'Well, it's a long story.'

'We could gather around and you tell us,' said a villager.

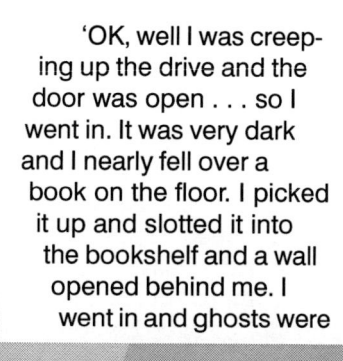

'OK, well I was creeping up the drive and the door was open . . . so I went in. It was very dark and I nearly fell over a book on the floor. I picked it up and slotted it into the bookshelf and a wall opened behind me. I went in and ghosts were fluttering around. I ran but fell into a trapdoor; it led me into a sewer full of rats. I cried for help, but no one came so I found a ladder to climb up and that's why I'm wet, cold and smelly now.'

'Come on, let's get you clean.'

After that day people never went near the house again. It was eventually demolished.

Serina Sidhu (9)

The Blacksmith And The Ghost

The blacksmith worked long hours and one night they really got to him or had they?

As he packed up for the night he heard footsteps. When he went to investigate, there, standing in front of him, was a young girl.

'Who are you?' he asked.

The girl raised her bloodied head and looked him in the eyes. 'Do not be afraid,' she said. 'I am . . . was Eleanor Cod.'

'What do you want with me?' he asked.

'I want revenge. Look, listen to my story. I lived with my uncle, Jack Cod, in Manchester on a farm. I worked there as the milkmaid until one day he told me that I had to leave. So his friend, John Sharp, collected me. He told me to follow him, which I did. We walked for what seemed like hours then he said he knew a 'short cut'. We walked across a field then stopped for the night. As I got comfortable he hit me on the head with his axe. He then threw my body in a pit along with the axe. There he left me. Will you help me to get justice?'

'Yes,' replied the blacksmith.

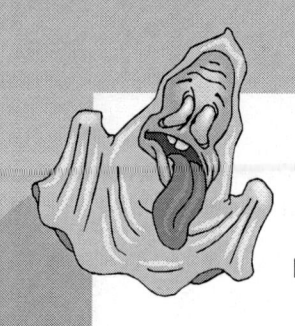

The next day Eleanor led the blacksmith to the place where she lay. He was horrified. He immediately told the police. Both men were guilty and sentenced to death. Now the blacksmith and Eleanor can rest in peace.

Charlotte Cooper (11)

Death With A Vengeance

The man licked the butler's blood off the small but deadly knife. He looked quite content with himself.

Kirsty woke with a fright. She breathed, her hands were all clammy and her head was hot. *It's all a dream,* she thought as she took a deep breath, *that wouldn't happen in real life.* Kirsty jumped, she heard screams coming from the kitchen. She ran down the winding tower to see what all the commotion was about.

Kirsty closed her eyes and then opened them again to see what she was seeing was real. Blood was dripping off the ceiling and walls, and knives were dug deep into the wall.

Kirsty dashed round the castle looking for help. Her shouts echoed through the empty castle. She ran down the stairs towards the basement. As Kirsty got nearer, she smelt a putrid smell. She turned the corner and lit a candle.

All around her were bodies pinned upon the walls. It was like some psychotic lunatic had stuffed all the bodies and hung them on the walls. The expressions on their faces looked helpless.

Kirsty felt someone's breath on the tip of her ear.

The man whispered in an icy tone, 'Tell them I kept my promise.'

She felt a sharp stab in her heart and all her blood was rushing to her head. She felt weak. The man looked pleased to see her squirming.

With her last ounce of breath she said, 'I love you Daddy.'

Kainaz Karkaria (14)

The School Ground Ghost

It was a normal school day when I was playing on the school ground with my friends, Tom and Harry.

We began to play tag. I started to chase Tom and Harry. I was getting so close to Tom, when he tripped up and went flying in the air. He had tripped up on a lump in the ground.

Harry ran up towards me; we didn't know how the lump appeared there because all the rest of the playground was flat.

Tom ran back up to us and said, 'We've got to dig that lump tonight.'

Harry and I agreed.

It was eight o'clock at night when we all met by the lump with our spades; we began to dig.

'We've dug half of the lump now,' said Harry.

As soon as Harry had finished his sentence, the lump started shaking and then it exploded. The whole lump was destroyed and out shot a man. His hair was an earthy mud pie, oozing with thick clods of decay. His mouth was covered with cold sores reaching up to his forehead. His nails were as long as pencils and as yellow as lemons. The man's stench was that of sour milk.

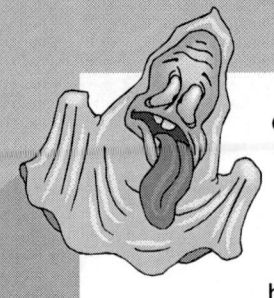

Suddenly the gruesome man yelled through his tortured face, 'Don't you dare disturb me again!'

As the man continued to shout, Tom and Harry scampered off home. I used my spade as a walking stick to follow them nervously home.

Jacob Matthews (11)

Lunar Relations

Lizzie Millar didn't care what her grandfather told her. There was nothing wrong with Lunar Wood and she could walk through it when there was a full moon if she liked. Lizzie was 12 years old and had honey-blonde hair. She was loud and confident and really couldn't care less about all the old superstitious claptrap her grandad was always rambling on about.

She'd just turned round and was returning home when she heard the sound of bleating sheep in the field on the left-hand side of the path. *Stupid animals,* thought Lizzie and she stopped to see what the commotion was about. At first she could see nothing, but she then spotted something in amongst the flock. Lizzie watched in horror as a mysterious, dark creature carefully separated one of the sheep. Within seconds it sped towards the innocent animal and ran it down. The creature then backed its head and uttered a blood-curdling howl of savage triumph. It lowered its head and then with an effortless gesture began to shred the corpse. Lizzie had already begun to walk quickly but quietly back up the path, still keeping her eyes on the creature. She felt the irresistible urge to run but something in her subconscious subdued this desire.

Suddenly something grabbed her hair. She screamed and thrashed her arms. Heart pounding, Lizzie got whatever it was off her hair and backed away and leaned on the fence behind her. She looked around for her attacker. To her astonishment it was the branches of a tree. Then she spun round and threw her hands over her mouth. Although its face was hidden, Lizzie knew it was looking at her. Instinctively now she ran and maybe it would have been better if she'd stayed to see what it did. As it saw the girl sprint along the path, the creature's hunting instinct and savage mind took hold. It gave chase.

Lizzie was almost at the end of the path and she wasn't alone, a snarl from behind her made Lizzie's feet pound harder on the ground and her brain go into overload. What in the world is that thing? She dodged a puddle and looked up into the sky. A full moon in perfect clarity shone down upon the blackened landscape. Then before she knew it, Lizzie fell. The werewolf was on her. Its teeth sunk into her shoulder and stabbing pain entered her body. She beat and kicked the monstrous hound but it was as if it didn't feel pain. Then she saw the Swiss army knife lying almost hidden by the mud. Instantly she grabbed it and slashed the knife across its right eye. The werewolf howled in pain and took off into the night, its screeches echoing through the forest.

Now as you probably know, those bitten by a werewolf, that live to tell the tale, also fall victim to the curse. A month after the attack, Lizzie had undergone the pain of becoming a werewolf. Poor Lizzie considered using the Swiss army knife that

A YOUNG WRITERS ANTHOLOGY

had saved her to now kill herself, but as the months went by, Lizzie began to enjoy being a creature tied to the moon.

Two months ago she brutally murdered her biggest rival Vicky and had not yet been identified. Her quest for blood had been a new and exhilarating experience. But little did she know that someone knew her secret and that someone was the very person that had bitten Lizzie in the first place.

It was about an hour before nightfall and Lizzie was already hiding in Lunar Wood awaiting the full moon that would release the beast in her. 'Waiting is such a bore,' she said.

'Isn't it so?' came a voice from behind.

She twirled round to see and who else but her own grandfather. His benevolent face beamed down towards her.

'What are you doing here?' Lizzie queried.

Her grandfather grinned.

Old duffer, thought Lizzie, *he might as well commit suicide as walk into a werewolf's lair.*

'I was here first,' he said.

Lizzie frowned. 'What is he on about?' she said to herself with mounting incredulity.

'I have been prowling these woods since before you were born!' he yelled.

Lizzie shivered. She wished he'd gone to a doctor about the scar over his eye. It was so creepy. She stopped. A scar on his right eye . . . she thought back to the attack. Lizzie pictured herself grabbing the knife and . . . she mouthed silently the words, 'I have been prowling these woods since before you were born'. These were the words that rang in her ears.

'That's right,' he chuckled.

'But . . .' Lizzie was lost for words.

'You are a threat to me,' the old man was smiling wildly. 'I must kill you,' he said quietly and with that, pulled out an old-fashioned pistol. She had always treated him like dirt, but now she'd pay!

The silver bullet hit Lizzie's heart. Birds took off, calling in alarm and the body of Lizzie Millar hit the ground. Five minutes later, a huge wolf with silvering fur could be seen stalking the path of Lunar Wood for those too foolhardy to heed the warnings of an old man.

Emma Baillie (13)

The Worst Nightmare

Two weeks ago, I was in my bedroom. I had just woken up from a very bad nightmare. I was all sweaty and out of breath. It might not have been a nightmare. I might have been in the graveyard. I'm pretty sure I was, because I felt and still do as though I lived it.

I heard a tapping on my window. It was not a normal tapping. I thought it was a human that had done it because an eerie voice called my name.

'Joe, Joe.'

I felt a cold chill going down my spine. I had felt scared and frightened, as a matter of fact I still am. I was scared because I was all alone because both my parents work night shifts. My parents are working the same hours so they don't get back for hours. Then I heard that voice again. My heart missed a beat.

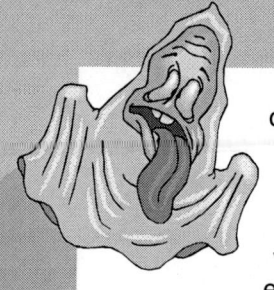

I heard my front door swing open. It could not have been my mum and dad back yet. It was only eleven fifty-five. I heard two rough, eerie voices, the ones that I heard when my windows were being tapped. I could hear the swishing of the people. If it was swishing it could only mean one thing.

My door banged down. I was looking at two ugly spectres, they were closing in on me. The clock struck twelve, the spectres vanished. Then I woke up. That was the worst nightmare ever. The nightmare still comes back to haunt me.

Joseph Mullen (13)

The Magical Lake

It all began in June. Sapphire and I wanted to go away for a break so we did. We went to a place called Fort William. There was a camping site at the bottom of Ben Nevis and a lake a quarter of the way up.

The first morning I woke up and Sapphire had gone. I thought she had gone for a walk. I went to look for her. I started to walk up the hill. I was near the lake and I heard laughing. It sounded like Sapphire. I ran as fast as a cheetah. I saw her. She was kissing someone and hugging him. I ran to the other side of the lake and I looked through my binoculars to see what they were doing. Then I knew who it was. William, her work colleague. I was so angry.

A hand came up from the water. I was terrified.

A voice came from the sky saying, 'Collect the book from the hand and read chapter 13.'

I did.

The book said: 'Bring the monster from the lake and say who you want to drown, read the next chapter and your wife will come back to you . . .'

I did as the voice said. I pulled the monster from the lake: it was massive, green and slimy. It started lumbering towards William.

I heard a scream. William was drowned. I read the next chapter quickly and Sapphire came back, forgetting what had happened.

But . . . I have a dreadful feeling that William will be back.

David James

The Man Werewolf

I am scared because a man werewolf has been chasing me for seven months. This might sound mad and crazy but I've seen it with my own eyes. At first I thought it was my imagination. I told my mum but she doesn't believe me. She just says that I'm seeing things. When I'm in my bed I can't sleep because I hear funny noises like growling and whispering mumbles that say my name.

One day I went to the library and I looked at a history book of a man who was cursed to be a creature of the dark world and so found eternal life. In 1592 a wizard called Andrew Toldson gave a man called Stuart Davidson a type of magic drink. Strangely, the article did not explain what happened to Davidson.

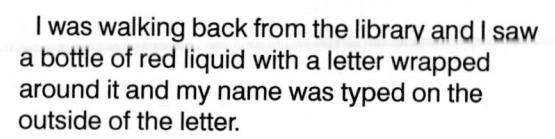

I was walking back from the library and I saw a bottle of red liquid with a letter wrapped around it and my name was typed on the outside of the letter.

I walked slowly towards the bottle and I opened the lid and took a smell of the red liquid. I knew it was blood. The letter said that he was going to get me like I got him. I had no idea who he was and I'd never 'got' anybody.

I was in my house when the front door swung open. I thought it was my mum but it wasn't. It was the man werewolf coming to get me for what I had done to him. I figured that he thought that it was me who'd turned him into the creature. I had not been dreaming and no one can help me . . .

Kevin Beurskens

The Chanting

We should never have done it. I realise now how stupid it was. It seemed like a good idea at the time.

My best friend's birthday party was really boring so I decided to liven it up a bit. No one believed in ghosts or evil spirits so I set up a Ouija board. I'd read about them and I knew what to do, so we started to play.

'I'll go first,' I said. I wasn't scared.

We put our fingers on the glass in the middle of the board. We started to chant this spell thing and that's when it all began .

'Devils of the dark, devils of the night, give us all a dreadful fright.' We must have chanted at least ten times. We didn't think anything was going to happen, when all of a sudden the electricity cut out. We lit a few candles but they didn't give off much light. We looked at the board on the floor, the glass started moving in a pattern. It read out the word *'death'*.

I started to panic and went to grab hold of a friend, when I realised they weren't there. I said their names but there was no reply.

All of a sudden the lights flickered back on again. Written on the board was a message. It read, *'for waking me up, you have to pay'*.

The payment was my friends.

Fiona Finlay (12)

Locked In (While Skipping School)

I shouldn't have been there in the first place. For once, I wished I was at school. To be able to press pause on the remote and calm down for a while. But I couldn't, this was real.

There I was, yanking at the door handle, but it just wouldn't budge. I knew I had to find another way out. I turned around and walked out of the room. Directly in front of me was a huge, oak-floored corridor. I'd never seen a walkway that big, except possibly at the airport. I started walking along. Every footstep I took echoed around me. It felt like being in a gigantic cinema, with speakers integrated into all the walls. Just ahead of me were some stairs. I went up them, intrigued to see what was there.

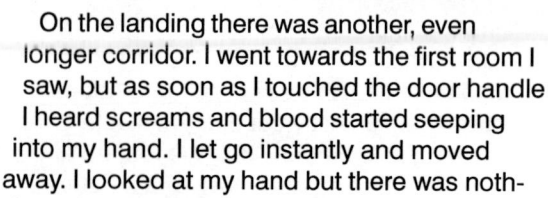

On the landing there was another, even longer corridor. I went towards the first room I saw, but as soon as I touched the door handle I heard screams and blood started seeping into my hand. I let go instantly and moved away. I looked at my hand but there was nothing there. I turned around and tried the handle on another door. It opened easily.

Inside was an exact replica of my bedroom. I ran over to my dog, but as soon as I stepped inside I started falling. Down and down, then it stopped and I was back in the kitchen. I tried the door, which opened and I ran away. Hopefully never to return.

Daniel Wieringa (13)

The Ghostly Room

Mum had liked the house for a while now, but somehow didn't like the look of it. The day soon came when she plucked up the courage to walk into the estate agents' and book an appointment to view it on 30th July.

The day soon came when we were leaving the house to go and view Churchyard Cottage, when suddenly the phone rang.

Running to the phone, I answered, 'Hello.'

'Don't go, don't go.'

I was about to take my next breath when suddenly the line went dead. Slowly, putting the phone down, I thought nothing of it at the time.

I sat in the car and the journey began. The words kept running through my head - 'Don't go, don't go'.

Soon we arrived at Churchyard Cottage. We knocked on the door for about five minutes. When it opened, strangely enough by itself. Mum and I looked at each other in shock.

We slowly walked in and there was no sign of the estate agent. Mum was eager to get started looking around. On the floor was shattered glass. We took a deep breath and wandered through the house. We went upstairs and straight into the first bedroom.

'*Aaarrrggghhh,*' we both screamed.

There in the corner was a girl, staring at us, saying, 'You disobeyed me. Punishment.'

We ran for the door. It suddenly slammed and locked. We both took a gulp and looked at the girl . . .

Amy Simpson (13)

The Wrong Place At The Wrong Time

'Lucy, Thomas, come on we're going. Got all your things? Say goodbye, this will be the last time you ever step foot into this house again, come on.'

'OK we're here now. Mum why do we have to leave Preston and go up to Manchester? It's just not fair!' snivelled Lucy.

Lucy scrambled into the car with her brother, Thomas, and finally the Benson family departed from their ancient semi-detached house.

Forty-five minutes later the Benson family arrived at 42 Middleton Road, Manchester, with an overloaded Range Rover, staggering up the spindly, spiral drive. As they approached the derelict mansion, Lucy suddenly yelled with horror. The petrified father jammed on the screeching car brakes and the car suddenly came to a halt.

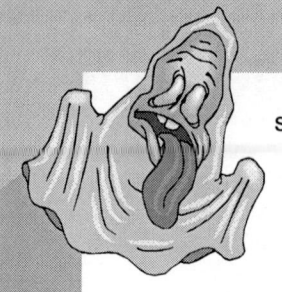

'What's the matter Lucy? Your father nearly killed us!'

'I . . . saw a black shadow glaring at me in that upstairs window.'

'Don't be ridiculous Lucy, it's probably just the clouds.'

The family drove on and just round the next twisty corner there it was, stranded in the middle of a dejected field, the mansion!

'There it is kids, look at it, it's going to be great.'

Lucy and Thomas were sitting there, examining the derelict house, when suddenly the car door flung open and there was their father sternly staring.

'The vicious door! Come on you two daydreamers, your mother and I are going to explore our new home, room by room. Isn't it great, come on.'

'Just one minute, see you in there.'

Alex Stephenson (13)

Ghost Story

It was a normal, cold London night, or so the underground cleaners thought it was. They hurried about business as usual and didn't notice the deep scratch marks in the back of the door.

Jackie bustled down the underground escalator, to get a broom from the cleaning cupboard. She felt a shiver run down her spine and felt that feeling of being watched. She quickly dismissed the idea, but didn't notice the beady red eyes staring down at her from the air vent.

As she closed the cleaning cupboard door she had that horrible feeling of being watched again.

Suddenly she felt claws ripping the flesh around her neck. She tried to scream, but had a dirty rag shoved in her mouth.

Early the next morning the tube driver walked into the station unaware of last night's events. He looked at his watch. 'Ten minutes early,' he said to himself. He had just enough time to get a snack from the vending machine. 'Damn! Stuck again!' The tube driver shook the vending machine as usual. To his horror a unrecognisable body fell out from behind the machine. It was so horrific he ran screaming, up the escalator and out of the scratched door.

Amber Heath (12) & Kirsty Baston (10)

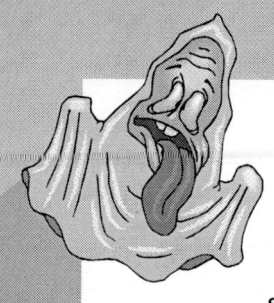

In The Barn

The stars and moon above were slowly disappearing behind a blanket of roaring clouds, leaving me in darkness. I felt a cold chill streak down my spine, as the wind was rattling the old and decrepit doors of the barn. I daren't go in. Being on my own, enclosed in a dark room with only one exit. No thank you.

As I sat down, on the cold, muddy ground, a bitter wind began whistling in my ears. Thunderous clouds from above were now hanging over me, roaring with immense loudness. When suddenly, a bolt of lightning plunged itself into the ground, only metres in front of me causing me to literally jump out of my skin.

From the newly burnt ground emerged a very frail-looking character. My heart began to race. Thumping hard against my chest. Who, or should I say, *what* was it? Whatever it was, its face looked as if it had been carved into the palest of stone. She wore long rags, which trailed on the floor, and her long, skinny body was floating inches off the ground. Next thing I knew, she started to approach me, as if in a trance she kept coming; slowlyl mysteriously.

I immediately turned and ran into the barn, slamming the door behind me. Hiding behind a bale of hay, I continuously stared at the door, hoping that what I thought might happen, didn't; but it did. The handle of the door twitched. I was trapped.

Nadine Rudd (13)

Just Another Piano Practice

Sheila knew from the start she didn't like the piano. Its white teeth glared at her, its bold frame filled her with fear, and something made her want to run as far from it as she could . . .

'It looks lovely Sheila, I knew it would,' beamed her dad. He hoped she would be the next Beethoven. 'Why don't you have a go on it?'

Sheila shivered. 'No thanks Dad.' She closed her eyes but the piano was still lurking in her mind, taunting her.

'Maybe later then.'

Sheila followed her dad out of the room - and closed the door behind them.

That night she had a nightmare about the piano and woke shaking with fear. She kept telling herself it was only a dream but she had the feeling the piano was waiting for her . . .

Two days later her dad was furious with Sheila. 'You haven't practised at all, and your lesson's tomorrow!' He locked her in the room despite the protests. 'You're not coming out until you practice,' he insisted, and left her alone . . . with the piano.

Sheila took a deep breath. 'I can do this. It's just another piano practice, that's all.' She perched on the piano stool and her heart beat faster and faster . . .

But she forced herself to place her sweaty fingers on those sinister white teeth, and began to play . . .

An hour later her dad opened the door - and Sheila wasn't there, but the piano grinned at him. It was satisfied - until it got hungry again.

Kerry Nesbitt (13)

A YOUNG WRITERS ANTHOLOGY

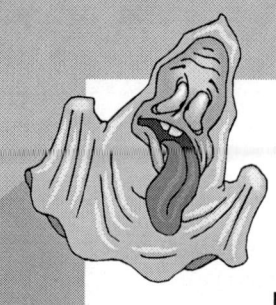

The Prisoner Of Alamar

As the embers of the flame-worn torch glowed a bitter red, the cold echo of footsteps beckon the dungeon floor and the tales of criminals linger in the air, surrounded by the stares of many empty eyes.

He walked to death as time and life was dragged from him. Should he pay for his crime; cruel as it was, would a punishment so harsh be equal for the families he tore apart? The ghosts of those he hurt and slaughtered now haunted his days.

The leaves fell to an end, so when in a day not even the stars can penetrate because this jailed man was set free...

It was 1829, Matthew and Marion Carpenter were embarking on the route they always took, walking through the Forest of Farland, as golden leaves bedded their path.

Matthew, a hardworking labourer, looked upon his caring housewife in a time where poverty and hardship could not overpower happiness. Their journey met the heart of the wood, where the air froze, for this is the same wood *he* used to pick his victims. They carried on not noticing the dark grey that was now the world.

The voices once talking, stopped. A blackened heart, cloaked and armed with sword and dagger crept out. His voice entitled to be accompanied by the hideous screeching of long ago banished wolves. Creatures of darkness. Their claws embedded in the snow. The tribe of the beasts were back . . .

Maria Goodhew (13)

Will You Scream?

Once upon a time there was a young boy called Jake. Jake's parents always told him not to worry about ghosts because they were not true. Jake's sister though was a right tease and told him all about how she had encountered a ghost whilst sitting on the toilet seat humming Gareth Gates' new release. Jake always feared the ghosts while planting his bottom down on the seat.

On one surprisingly chilly day, Jake heard a loud smash coming from halfway down the toilet. Jake shivered - a magical spirit flew down his spine which made him jump.

'Who's down there? Don't make me use this toilet plunger.'

Suddenly a white figure scooted from out of the toilet and pirouetted right in front of Jake's face.

'Who are you?' asked Jake suspiciously.

The ghost didn't reply but did turn around and show Jake his back.

'Ooh, now that's creepy.'

Millions and millions of maggots fled from the ghost's back and started to cover Jake. He squirmed and squiggled trying to release himself from the maggots. Soon Jake felt a tap on his left shoulder, it was his sister. Jake had fell into a deep sleep on the toilet and was just recovering when he heard his mum's voice from downstairs.

'Jake, dinner's ready.'

Jake ran downstairs half expecting to see his mum placing a full English breakfast on the table, but to his horror he saw maggots being placed in a stew brewing on the table.

Scott Bacon (11)

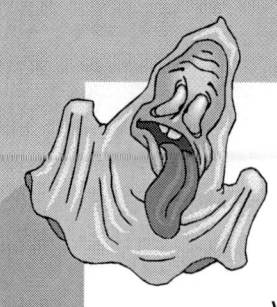

Ghost Story

Three years ago I was at Jeromima's house. His house is massive, people called it Whitburn. I was at his garden gate, it was big. I walked into his garden, it was very posh, I got to his door.

Jeromima answered the door and said, 'Come in.'

I walked in, it had a green and brown carpet, the stairs were windy, the walls were blue with loads of pictures of old people.

His house looked strange. When I was in his house the doors were squeaking and the blinds were moving, it was warm.

I asked him for a drink, he poured it for me, it was very cool and refreshing, he told me to go upstairs, so I was walking up the stairs and the temperature dropped, it was cool so I kept walking, it went back to normal temperature and I went into his room.

It was time for me to go home so I said, 'Jeromima, it's time for me to go now, see you later.'

I was walking back down the stairs when at the same place again the temperature dropped so I shouted, 'Jeromima you need to turn the heating on on the stairs.'

All of a sudden Jeromima ran out of his bedroom and down the stairs and out the door.

I ran after him but he was gone, so I went to look for the heater, I turned the heating right up and went to the stairs and the temperature was still cool.

Now I know what Jeromima would not tell me or anyone.

Lee Allen (12)

Carnival Spectacular

The empty swings clattered and the chimes twined in the hard wind. The candyfloss stalls were shattered and the 'loopy loop' roller coaster groaned loudly. Noise after noise whirled around and around and around in one big circle, the area changing place after place. Clown advertisement light ups were talking, laughing, joking; scary.

They had come, taking many lost lives with no warning. What had been a happy, cheerful carnival turned into a deadly trap. I mean it was there, staring in people's faces. Who would set up a carnival in the middle of the freezing season? Them, them of course, trapping us to a deadly death.

The horrors of the graves and below, the Earth slowly weakening by their great numbers; had struck, an expected attack. The people knew in Las Modena that they'll come one day, uninvited. And what better place to start it, at the carnival, where many people go to have fun, but this time it was to scream in horror. Blood and intestines were splattered across mazes, mirrors, any possible space. And there in a dark corner, behind the stripy circus tent, was Asmiranda, crouching low, keeping into the deadly shadows that surrounded her, lost, lost in confusion and devastation.

Her beady hazel eyes patrolled around her position, scanning every dark corner, as far as her eyesight would let her look.

Asmiranda looked down on her stinging

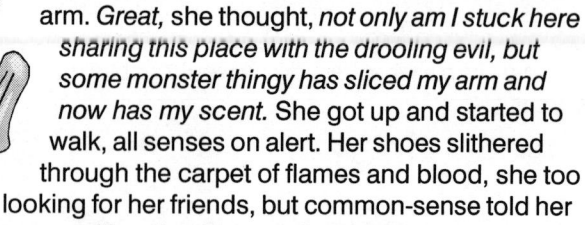

arm. *Great,* she thought, *not only am I stuck here sharing this place with the drooling evil, but some monster thingy has sliced my arm and now has my scent.* She got up and started to walk, all senses on alert. Her shoes slithered through the carpet of flames and blood, she too looking for her friends, but common-sense told her that this was neither the time nor the place.

Coming towards the giant blue iron gates, Asmiranda heard a shuffle that sounded too close for comfort. She whizzed around and saw a pair of red eyes, staring intently at her. Her heart was then pounding so hard that she was surprised that it didn't burst out of her chest, her knees feeling like jelly; trembling to the gravelled ground, weakening to the powerful eyes. A claw gnashed out, cutting her throat open in the process. The spider-like creature, bringing down its right claw out; got stopped halfway by a piece of wood, blocking its path to its sweet revenge.

Asmiranda punctured the splintering wood through the stomach, until she was satisfied that it was in as far as she could possibly push it through and fled, knowing that it would not keep it for very long.

Running through the ghostly shadows and dim lights that towered over her, Asmiranda was wanting so much to be home, but would it still be home? Would it still be there? Pounding through the darkened alley, she finally reached the back door. They obviously hadn't reached the city yet.

Everything seemed to be in place. Banging heavily on the oak door, Asmiranda's mum answered, looking terrified and white in the face, before she collapsed in a heap on the green tiled floor. And what do you know? There, stood behind her was her beloved dad, yellow fiery eyes dancing at her in glee.

'What's the matter dear, you look like you've just seen a . . . vampire!'

Georgina Ann Evans (13)

The Strange But Posh House

I was just visiting my friend because she'd just bought a mansion. She hadn't seen me for a long time. I started to get excited.

When I arrived her grass was well cut. Her flowers were so pretty. The drive was well paved. Her house was absolutely huge. I couldn't believe my friend Ruby had turned out to be a millionaire.

When the door opened she didn't seem to be so happy to see me.

'What's wrong Ruby?' I asked.

'N-n-nothing,' she replied.

'Are you sure?' I said.

She nodded and showed me in.

Her hall carpet was an eyesight. It had silver, grey, black, red and peach colours. Her hall was brown and red. I could tell something was wrong. I needed to find out what.

As we were watching a movie, I heard a noise from the corner of the room. I walked up to the second floor. I saw the bedroom door close.

I stepped into the room, then I looked back and saw it. I know now what Ruby does . . .

Naomi Payne (11)

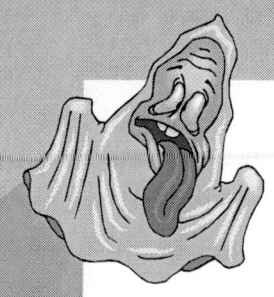

Gory Mansion

One sunny day in the summer I was off to visit my aunty's new mansion as I would be staying over this summer due to my parents being away.

I walked up Westoe village and came to my aunt's mansion, called Westoe Hall. I felt nervous staying at her new place. It looked old but strong and proud.

The door opened and my aunt Sabrina opened the door and welcomed me in. I looked around the entrance hall, it had two sets of staircases on either side. It was Victorian with candles and dark paintings.

'Let me show you to your bedroom,' said my aunt kindly.

'Sabrina, did you decorate this place yourself?' I asked.

'Yes I did, do you like it?' she replied.

I didn't answer, I thought it looked awful. Then Sabrina opened a door and started crying.

'Oh my baby girl Bonnie was murdered in this very room,' sobbed Sabrina.

'But I thought Bonnie was my age Aunty?' I questioned.

She didn't answer and led me next door, then stopped.

'Whatever is wrong Aunt Sabrina?' I asked cautiously.

'Nothing darling,' she said to me.

I suddenly felt a gush of coldness and Sabrina escorted me into the room.

'This room is a little drafty Sabrina.'

She left me in the room and I went to bed. I decided to explore. I walked up dark stairs, and there she was floating in the light shining through the window. *It's her, it's her*, I just couldn't believe it.

Jasmin Turner (11)

Third Floor Bathroom

My friend Izaak and me were sleeping over at my grandma's that night. She had something on her mind. Then she warned me about the third floor bathroom.

It was 11 o'clock, I couldn't get to sleep because of what she said, so I went downstairs to get a drink. It was freezing. When I went upstairs I told Izaak that the following day we would see what she meant. All night I stared at the roof. I was tired in the morning and I reminded Izaak about that night.

That night I had tea and went to bed, waiting for 12 o'clock so I could go to see what she meant about the third floor bathroom.

Me and Izaak crept upstairs, I got colder at every step, it was like minus twenty-four. I went pale and I hadn't seen anything, yet every step I got closer to seeing what she meant.

I was at the second floor. I started to hear creaks on the third floor. I was absolutely freezing. I was on the third floor looking right at the bathroom waiting to see what she meant. I turned the handle of the door, I looked inside and I saw nothing, I was disappointed really. I turned around and I fainted.

A YOUNG WRITERS ANTHOLOGY

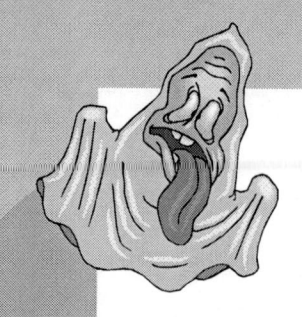

Now I know what she meant about the third floor bathroom. And I will never go to that bathroom again.

Alex Knight (11)

The Man On The Ground Floor

It was last year during my holiday in France when I saw him. I haven't been the same since. We were at an exclusive four star hotel called the Exotic Princess. We were staying in Room 427, two rows from the top and the hotel seemed really nice. The people too were pleasant enough. You know how I said I was never the same again? Well, now I will tell you why.

We had been at the hotel for two days and by this time I knew my way around. The hotel kept on having strange power cuts and no one seemed to know why, although no one said anything about it. We had just arrived at the restaurant when my mum told me she had forgotten her purse. I said I would go back to the room to get it and headed for the lift. I wish now that I hadn't volunteered.

Although the hotel was modern, it had a strange atmosphere. It felt like someone was always there, watching you. I pressed the button for the lift and when the doors opened, I stepped inside and pushed the button for level 4. The lift began to move but then stopped suddenly with a slight jerk. Then the lights went out. All of a sudden I felt the lift plummeting downwards. I screamed as red lights flashed all around me. Then the lift stopped and the doors opened to reveal a damp and eerie room. I looked around, but all I could see were mops and buckets. Then I saw him, a shadow lurking in the corner. The shadow rose and came towards me, but I dared not get out of the lift. I panicked...

I woke up flat on my back on the lift floor. To this day I don't know or remember all of what happened, just that I don't want to stay in French hotels ever again.

Nicole Atkinson (12)

Keera's Spooky Kitchen

I started at the gates, I passed the flowers to the front door. Keera answered, I gave her her birthday flowers. This day was the day of her twelfth birthday.

She said, 'Go straight up the stairs.'

I asked her, 'Why is the party upstairs?'

She said, 'I don't know.'

I also asked her why wasn't it in the kitchen like usual, and Keera said that she didn't know. So I secretly snuck downstairs and went in to the kitchen. When I went in, I felt a sudden rush of coldness, the coldness was mostly on the right hand side of me.

I asked her why her kitchen was so cold and Keera said that I shouldn't have gone in the kitchen. Keera said that many things will happen to me, like my life will be ruined forever.

Two weeks later, Keera got the house sold and moved to another country, and later on in my life, I had bad things happen to me, for example there was a nasty ghost following me.

What else do you think will happen in my life?

Craig Lyons (12)

A YOUNG WRITERS ANTHOLOGY

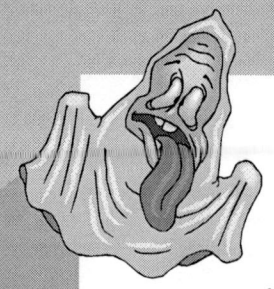

The Haunted House

Two years ago there was a boy called John and a girl called Kate, both 11 years old. On October the 31st, they had decided to sneak into the haunted house at the top of the street. As they walked closer, it was getting colder and colder. There were no street lights on, therefore it was very difficult to see. Kate and John held onto each other as they approached the house. When they finally reached the house, John and Kate were a little bit scared at first, but still walked through the door. The door closed after them with a *bang*.

The house was very cold and it had lots of cobwebs on the lights, windows and walls. The floor was just all wood with dust, and you could see footprints on it. The fireplace, which stood against the wall, was full of logs inside and on the top were photos of a family.

Suddenly there was a shadow running. John screamed and ran outside, then Kate followed him. As they ran out, all the windows shattered and the doors slammed shut behind them. Kate and John ran as fast as they could back to their own home, shaking with fear. As Kate told her mam about what happened, her mam just laughed at her. She didn't believe her story and told her not to make things up, as her imagination was unbelievable.

Emma Steele (11)

Help!

It was our first night in our new house and we were both asleep, but then . . .

'What was that!' cried Ant.

'I don't know, it sounded like someone screaming,' I said.

'Heeeelp meeee, heeeelp,' muttered a soft voice.

Me and Ant sat there terrified. It was our new house, so it made it even worse.

Then we saw her. She had jet-black hair and a long nightie on, and she was crying. Ant looked like he was about to cry too.

'Have you seen my mum?' she said.

'No,' I said.

Then she disappeared and we heard another scream.

'Help me, he is hurting me,' she cried. Then she appeared again. 'Please, my dad killed me and my mum, and he is still hurting me.'

Then someone who looked like her mum came running towards us, carrying a Bible. She told Ant to read a sentence, so he did. Then there was a flash and the man was gone. Then they hugged each other, said thank you to us and walked away through the wall. Then I woke up. It was all a dream I thought. I leant over to Ant to tell him about it, but then I saw the Bible.

James Lees (13)

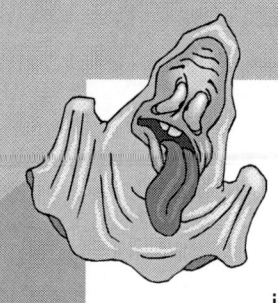

I'll Be Back . . . For You!

Hello, my name is Victoria Carlsworth. I live on the outskirts of London in a small town called Dawn's Dale. It is very peaceful, but this is also where my story begins.

About ten years ago on a cold, dark, winter's night, me and my brother Harry had been playing in the library, and that's when it happened. Our ma and pa had gone to a wedding and we had been left with our Nanny Clara.

There was a knock on the door. The knock was so loud it seemed to make the whole house shudder. Clara rushed to the door. She opened it, but saw no one, so she went back to cooking our supper.

Again we heard the knock and this time when Clara opened the door, something terrible must have happened, because we heard a blood-curdling scream come from the kitchen and four seconds later, a thud.

As we ventured towards the kitchen we turned on the hall lights and walked cautiously to the kitchen door. I pushed the door very slowly, trying not to make the door creak. I turned on the light and screamed in horror at what I saw. There was blood all up the walls, on the floor, on the door, in the sink. It was everywhere and there in the corner was Clara's head, with at least thirty slashes in it. It was then I saw the words on the wall, in blood! 'I'll be back . . . for you!'

Sophie Moran (12)

Her!

On a dark, dreary night I found myself walking along the cobbled, windy road towards the huge carcass of a mansion with lightning crashing over it. When I came to the towering doors I grasped the large lion head door knocker and banged it against the door once, twice. Although I feared to knock again I did, this time slightly quieter. One door pulled open on its own and crashed behind me. I started to climb the huge staircase. As I did, I saw her coming up behind me, so I followed. I passed through three dark, damp rooms and finally came to a small room with a tall, cobwebbed, spiral staircase. I knew having come this far I couldn't turn back, so I clutched the dusty rail and stopped. As I climbed, I could hear faint child's giggling echoing around me.

At the top, there was a small, wooden, dusty door. I could see some markings on the bottom and the corner of the door looked scratched and cracked, like someone had been frantically trying to escape. I carefully dusted the markings and read, 'D-E-A-T-H'. *Death*. I then found a large crack at the top of the door, so reluctantly I peered in. 'Argh!' I let out an ear-piercing scream. She was there, hanging from the ceiling, with a tight, thick rope around her neck!

Lisa Hine (12)

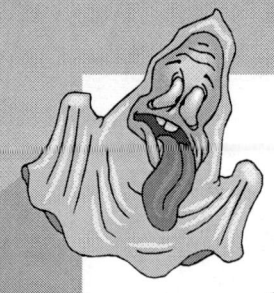

The Fictional Painting

It was the eyes in the painting following me, those red, gleaming eyes. Everywhere I went they went, it was like they were waiting for me. I even asked to be moved into a different room, but it was like the painting wouldn't let me. It was like I didn't even have a soul for myself.

I lay in bed and I could hear voices saying, *'Beware of the stroke of midnight.'* Suddenly, I heard footsteps, squeaking footsteps coming down the hall. The noise was unbearable, they seemed to be coming towards me, but how? There was no one else around me. Then I heard a squeaking door and I could feel a cold breeze coming towards me. I was ice-cold and I couldn't move. Then I heard the stroke of midnight from my great big grandfather clock. *Ding, ding,* then there was silence. Someone grabbed me from behind and got a grip on my stiff neck. It tried to pull me out of my bed towards the painting. It was too strong for me, it was pulling me towards the painting. Closer and closer I went. I tried squirming to get free from its muscular hand, but by then it was too late, it had pulled me into the painting. I was horrified. All I could see now was whiteness, pure whiteness. I thought, *what should I do? From here and now I'm just waiting, just waiting for someone to save me.*

Daniel Shore (12)

Can't Escape

I was trapped, I couldn't get out. There were people's voices saying, 'You can't escape.' I saw something move in the hallway, I quickly ran to a table and hid behind it. It suddenly vanished. I got up and kept on walking down the dark hallway. I heard footsteps coming from the stairs. I cautiously walked towards the stairs, there was nobody there. I walked upstairs. There were five doors on each side. I went to the first door, it was locked, so were all the others, except for the last door. I went in. Looking around, there was another door. I slowly walked up and opened the door and walked in. I looked around and in the far corner of the room on the table, there was a key. I ran up to it and picked it up. I ran as fast as I could to the front door. When I got there, I saw a ghost. I froze. It was standing in front of the door. I shouted, 'I am not giving up now.' I ran straight at the ghost and put the key in the hole and turned the knob. The door opened. I ran out, slamming the door behind me.

Nathan Monks (13)

The Girl In The Attic

I had just moved into my new house, that's when it all started.

The doors upstairs would move slightly of their own accord and a soft sort of crying would come from the attic. So I would go up and the crying would stop, but there would be a soft, ice-cold breeze. And this would happen every night about then.

So I decided to ask some of the local people about the house, and I told them about the crying in the attic, but every single person would say something like, 'I don't know' or, 'It's probably just the wind'. But I didn't think so somehow, I couldn't explain even to myself why, but I was sure it was more than that.

Then I decided to go to the library. I asked the librarian if there were any books on ghosts in the local area. She pointed to a shelf with one fat book that looked like it had never been touched. I started to look down the contents page. There was my address, 29 Cobble Lane. I started to read. As I flicked through the pages, every page I turned was more horrifying.

There was a girl of about six years old who was beaten and tortured by the gardener and locked away in the attic. She would lie there crying for her mother, but they never found her.

I slammed the book shut and ran home. I knew what I had to do . . .

Charlotte Cotterill (13)

Tuppences

'Tuppences . . . have you got your tuppences?'

Josie awoke in a shock. She couldn't get the words out of her head.

'Tuppences, have you got your tuppences?'

All because of one night, a night to remember. It was seventeen years ago to the day. Or should I say the night?

'Josie, don't forget your tuppences,' said Harriet.

'Tuppences, why do

I need tuppences?' asked Josie.

'Oh I'll tell you later, just don't forget them!'

The girls got in the car and waited till they arrived at Elderflower Manor.

'Right girls, the other Brownies are in their dormitories, so why don't you go and join them? Snowy Owl, please could you show the girls their dormitories?' announced Brown Owl.

Josie and Harriet followed Snowy Owl along many corridors until finally they got to room 17.

'Great,' said Harriet as she flung the door open.

'There's only two of you in this room girls! Think yourselves lucky. Dinner will be served in 30 minutes, so in that time you can unpack your bags, can't you.'

'Yes Miss,' replied Josie.

Snowy Owl flung the door open and marched down the corridor.

'Josie, remember your tuppence. You know what will happen if you don't,' reminded Harriet.

'Tuppences . . . what do you mean?' replied Josie, but when she looked back, Harriet had gone.

Late that night when all lights were out, Harriet was sound asleep, but Josie was awake, getting her tuppence ready for him just as she was told to. She placed it under her pillow and fell asleep.

'Tuppences . . . have you got your tuppences?'

'Argh!' screamed the two girls.

Ellie Carding (13)

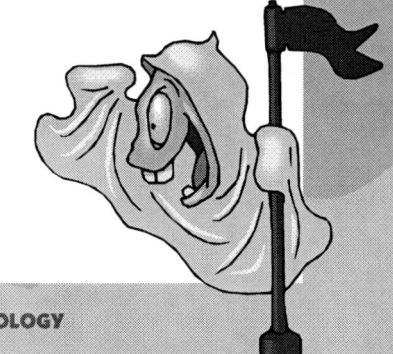

Trapped

It was just a normal, sunny day, or so that's what Jayne thought. Until it happened . . .

Jayne woke up bright and early, ready to greet the day. She went downstairs to find no one there. *That's odd,* she thought. Her mum was definitely not at work and would have told her if she was going out. 'Mum?' she called. No reply. 'Mum?' she called again a little louder, starting to panic. *Where is she?* she thought. She searched the house, but only to find it as empty.

Her mother and her lived together, just the two of them. All other family had either died or moved away. All they had now were friends. She picked up the phone ready to call someone. *But who?* she thought. She put the receiver down and decided she would be better off trying to find her mum herself. She quickly got dressed and went to the front door ready to leave to look for her mum. She turned the handle and pulled the door, but it wouldn't open. She tugged at it again, but it still wouldn't open! Soon she realised it was locked, but not from the inside, from the outside! Now she was locked in. Panicking, she ran to the phone and started to dial 999, but the phone was dead, the wires to it had been cut. Then she heard footsteps.

'Mum!' she shouted, but there was no reply. Tears started to stream down her face and she was shaking from fear. She ran to a window and tried to pull it open, but it was locked as well. She tried another one, but that was locked too. *I know,* she thought, *the key to the windows is down in the basement.* Now a bit excited, she ran down to the basement. She got down there and looked for the cupboard where the key was, but then she heard the door behind her slam shut. She screamed and pulled at the door trying to open it, but it was locked. Now she was really trapped.

The basement was cold and dark. Jayne was crying again by this time. She heard footsteps again. 'Who's there?' Jayne screamed. No reply. And then she felt a hand on her shoulder. She screamed. The hand didn't move though, but it gripped tighter.

Then she heard a voice, it said, 'Why did you come here?'

But Jayne screamed again. She ran to the door even though she couldn't quite find her way, but she did. The hand was still on her shoulder, but the door was unlocked. She pulled it open and ran out, but she wasn't in her house anymore, at least she thought she wasn't, and then she saw it . . . !

Sarah Woods (13)

Truth Or Dare

'It's your turn Dave,' said Emma.

John thought of a dare. 'I dare you to go into the haunted house across the road.'

'I'll die in there, please don't send me in,' replied Dave.

'Go on, it's not scary,' assured Emma.

Dave walked down the path and across the road. It was getting dark, it was getting scary. Dave walked through the gate, no one had lived in the house for ten years. Dave stepped inside quietly. There was a spiral staircase on his right, he could hear some tapping noises from upstairs, but he didn't take much notice of them. Dave crept through the wide hallway into the kitchen. There on the side was a mouth-watering pizza. He went up to it and it was still warm. Dave thought to himself, *there must be someone here.* A shiver went down his spine.

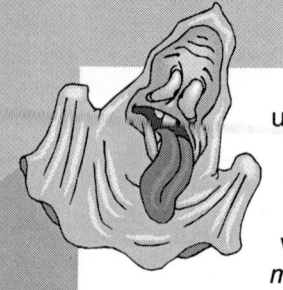

Dave walked up the spiral stairs. He heard a tapping noise again. Dave tiptoed up to the bedroom, it had a rocking chair in the corner, it was going forwards and backwards. Dave turned around and started to walk out of the room. 'Argh!' he shouted. There was a ghost at the door. Dave sprinted out of the room and down the stairs and tried to open the front door. The door was jammed. The ghost caught up with him and Dave fainted.

No one saw Dave after that day, and no one went in the house again.

Dan Byron (13)

The Greed Within

At the top of the path, the mansion was visible, hulking, looming, casting the ground around it into shadow. Robert squared his shoulders and began to navigate his way through the tangle of weeds. Finally, he reached the front door and pushed it open.

He was in the hallway of the mansion. Above him hung a huge and ornate candelabra, and to his right and left was a flight of curving stairs. Where the two flights met a passageway led into the gloom of the upper floor.

Now Robert began to regret the rash boast he had made to the patrons in his father's tavern. 'I will rid the village of this evil,' he had said. But what could he do? He was only a boy, an eighteen-year-old boy. Unfortunately, the rain had grown worse, and there was no way that he could return to the village that night.

Tentatively, Robert began to explore. He opened doors, he disturbed piles of dust. Then he came to another set of doors. They were blue, laced with intricate designs in gold. He pushed them open. With a creak, they gave. And what he saw chilled him to the bone. He had discovered the real reason that the Villefort family had disappeared. They had been murdered. And he had found their rotting corpses. Sitting there around the table, as if ready to eat a meal they would never see, their white bones gleaming and their eyeless skulls turned towards him.

Emma Wong (14)

The Ghost Of Floral Cottage

I am going to tell you the story of a ghost, a ghost called Thing. He lives within the cottage and feeds on the people which live in the house. For the past thirty years, people have lived there, but have survived no more than six months. He prefers children because he can shape-shift into anything he wants and can come out of a small crack in the floor as a clown.

One of the incidents happened just over a year ago when the Parker family moved into the cottage. They had a very big family which consisted of three kids and two adults.

The middle child, named Megan, came home from school one day and went to explore her new house. She went to the bedrooms and the kitchen, then the rest of the house, but not the basement, for her dad had heard noises down there and did not think it was safe.

Being a child, she ignored her dad and went to have a look. Slowly she went down the stairs and into the gloomy room. After work, her parents came home and could not find her so they called the police. They found her down in the basement with a rope around her neck and no arms or legs. One of the men swore that he saw a thing running away, but no one else saw it but him and the other two children.

Bryony Willis (12)

Victim

Walking through the dark street, she heard footsteps. She stopped. The footsteps stopped a split second after hers. Unnerved she carried on. She tried to keep in the dim glow of the streetlights that struggled to make themselves shown through the damp, cloying fog. Her footsteps were muffled, so the echoes she could hear were not from her own feet. She stopped again. Once more, the footsteps behind her carried on for a micro-second longer, then stopped, hiding in the shadows.

Steeling herself, she turned around and stared through the thick blanket that covered the streets. She could make no sense of the dim shapes that loomed out of the mists. There? A tree. Over there! Just a mail box. A movement! Just a cat running across the road. She walked on, a bit quicker now. She was almost home, she told herself, almost there. Then a thin, bony hand descended hard on her shoulder. She jumped, heart thudding wildly. She whirled around to face her attacker. It was a thin, pale man in a black suit.

The last thing the man saw was a woman with white skin, blood-red eyes and lips curled back to reveal two unnaturally long and sharp canines. Then there was just blood and pain.

He had only wanted directions.

Amber Curtis (14)

The Ghost Frog

One evening as the fire burned and the thunder cracked, Ashley sat in the living room in front of the fire eating her tea. Suddenly she heard two taps on the window and three different voices.

'Come.'

'Come.'

'Come.'

Ashley wanted to see what was at the window but every time she looked at the big, tall, wide windows she shivered and shook.

As time passed, Ashley heard more noises and more taps on the window. Ashley had had enough. She looked out the window. Nothing was there. She turned around. There in front of her was a big ugly frog. She took it to her bedroom and put it into an old cage which her hamster used to live in.

In the morning she looked in the cage that the frog was in. It was gone. She searched the whole house.

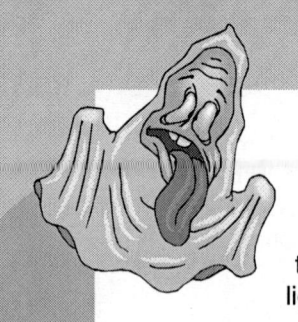

At midnight she woke up because she had a bad dream about a ghost - a ghost with one blue eye and one green eye and guess what was in front of her? A ghost frog! She quickly turned the light on. It was gone just like a bit of light the ghost frog disappeared.

The next night she turned the torch on and the frog flew out the window. The night after that she dropped five ice cubes on it and it froze. She threw it out the window and that was the end of the ghost frog and nobody saw the ghost frog ever, ever, ever again.

Amy Mason (9)

The Friendly Ghosts

Laura and Jack did not like their new house - but their mum stopped them from moving.

The next day Jack heard someone say, 'Boo!' *What can it be?* Jack thought. Jack got closer and he looked in his closet. 'What on earth is that?' Jack said in shock.

'Laura, Laura, wake up, there's a ghost in the house!'

'What do you mean?' asked Laura.

'It's the ghost,' answered Jack.

'For once I believe you, Jack.'

'Thank you very much.'

'I think it's moving towards us, Jack,' cried Laura. 'Mam.'

'What do you want?' shouted Mam.

'There's a ghost,'

replied Laura.

'Stop playing tricks on me, children,' said Mam crossly when she arrived upstairs.

Their mam went back downstairs.

'Hello,' said the ghost. 'Can I play with you?'

'We're not playing anything,' said Laura and Jack together.

'I'm really sorry for scaring you two,' said the ghost sadly.

'That's fine,' said Laura shakily. 'Who are you?'

'I'm Caspar. I've lived in this house for years,' said the ghost, 'and so have all my friends.'

After a little while, they all got on very well and Mam started to get the hang of it, and they never told anyone about the ghosts. Jack and Laura did not want to move house anymore now they had all the ghosts to play with.

Melissa Kelly (8)

Lost

The Smiths were driving through a dark, misty night. They were going on holiday in the Lake District. The countryside they were driving through became darker. Dad finally admitted that he was lost.

He stopped where a narrow road was leading towards a light. Dad got out the car and so did Mam, John and Oliver.

'We'd better ask directions,' said Dad.

They all started to walk towards the light.

The path turned to grass and suddenly John

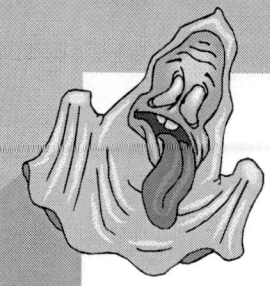

noticed that they were in a graveyard. Without warning a door appeared before them. Dad knocked and a strange man opened it.

'Follow me,' was all he said.

They reached an empty room where a candle burned.

'Wait there,' said the strange man and disappeared.

Out of nowhere ghostly goblins appeared and started dancing around them. The family was terrified. In the corner a box that looked like a coffin creaked open. A bony hand with dirty fingernails crept out of it and grabbed the edge of it. A shadow moved behind it.

'I don't want to see what comes next,' screamed Mam. She grabbed Dad's hand and that of Oliver who held John.

They ran as quick as the wind back to the car and Dad drove off with a loud roar. They heard a blood-curdling howl behind them.

'I'm glad we did not stay to be a vampire's dinner,' said Oliver to John shakily.

Charlotte Ditch (9)

The Unexpected Mystery

Kate invited me and some other friends over for tea. As I walked there a suspicious thing passed by. It was like a breeze heading for my friend's home. I ran as fast as I could but I could not catch up with it. It was like some wind in a tiny place that felt as if I was supposed to catch it.

I came close enough to make it out. At that moment I thought I might be in danger, it was like a slime *ghost!* But it was strange, I was not frightened. So, because I was desperate to get something to eat, I said calmly to myself, 'I'll go and get something to eat then check it out properly.'

After tea my friend and I stepped out of the house. The mysterious wind was waiting. It surrounded us.

A voice said, 'Help me!'

'How?' I asked.

The voice replied, 'Take me to the church.' There at my feet lay a lump of disgusting looking green slime repeating, 'Are you going to listen to me or not?'

I picked it up and took it to the church. My friend was scared.

Our feet moved as if we could not control them at all. When we got there we opened the door, ran in and put it down on the stone slabs. There was a flash and it went to Heaven.

A voice said, 'Thank you!'

Emma Wilson (8)

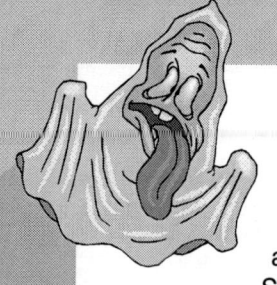

The Haunted Castle

One cold night there was a little cottage in the dark, dark woods. In there were two children and their parents. The two girls were called Sally and Jane, they were sent into the woods to pick some berries. Their mam said to come back at 3 o'clock.

When they were in the woods, Sally said, 'I don't like this. What was that noise?'

Jane said quickly, 'I don't know.'

Jane tripped over but Sally didn't notice, she carried on walking. Then Sally heard a big scream. It was Jane. She was taken into a dark, creepy old castle. It started to rain. Sally looked behind her and saw a creepy old castle, then realised that Jane was gone. She screamed! Sally ran to the castle because she didn't know her way back.

Jane saw Sally and shouted for her, 'Sally, Sally, help me!'

Sally said, 'I'm coming.'

The vampire took Jane in a room with big cobwebs and lots of creepy crawly spiders, bugs, worms and little things like that. Sally saw the vampire take her in, so she went as well. The door shut with a loud slam! She saw a big ghost right in front of her. She ran to the room where Jane was. The vampire looked up sharply.

He said in a loud voice, 'I am going to drink your blood for my dinner tonight.' He left with a slam of the door.

Sally had a plan to

get her hairband and tie it onto Jane's long belt. They got out of the castle but as soon as they got out of the castle, two big wolves jumped up on top of them and they were never seen again.

Samantha Hardy (8)

The Red Doll

Jenny had just moved into a 100-year-old mansion. She slowly walked over to the ten foot door and slipped in. Jenny gently pushed open the door to her room. In the room was a dressing table, four-poster bed and two wardrobes. Jenny went in and lay on the soft linen bed. Dazed, she fell asleep.

Jenny was awoken by the wind howling against her window. She jumped up, stretched and started to unpack. When she finished she made her way up to the attic. There was a musty smell inside. In the corner, Jenny noticed a red chest. She lifted the lid. In it was a box. Jenny tucked it under her jumper and ran to her room.

It was the fifth day at the mansion and Jenny's dad and the dog had been mysteriously murdered. Jenny felt it was now time to reveal what was in the box from the attic. She lay on the bed and opened it. A cloud of dust came out There was a Victorian doll.

'Jenny, time for bed,' shouted Mum.

She climbed into bed, put the doll down and fell asleep. Suddenly she woke up. Something was crawling up her. That was the last of Jenny.

Next day, Jenny's mum looked in and what met her eyes was a pile of bones which was once her little girl. Jenny's mam went mad and had to be put in hospital. This was the end of Jenny's family and the mansion. It was burned down to ashes.

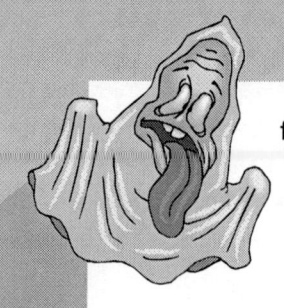

So, be careful where you go 'cause you might bump into something unexpected.

Ellen Lily Colling (9)

The Wicked Doll

Joe's, Jake's and Richard's mam and dad came home from their weekend holiday. They brought a singing Action Man for them.

The boys played and played with this toy. They loved it and always hated the night-time because instead of playing they had to go to bed. Richard didn't care and stayed up. As he played he got frightened because the Action Man sang to him, 'I will kill you'. Richard didn't like that.

Richard went and got a drink. The doll appeared halfway up the stairs with a knife. Richard carried on back up the stairs and off to bed. The doll felt cold as it climbed into bed with him and stabbed him ten times until he was dead.

That night the ghostly Action Man doll made sure that the same happened to Joe, Jake and their dad. Their mam suddenly woke up startled when the Action Man's blood-covered knife hovered above her head.

'You're next,' the quiet, menacing voice said.

Mam grabbed the doll and threw it at the wall with all her strength. The gruesome doll shattered into 1,000 pieces.

Richard, Joe, Jake and their dad came back to life. The boys never touched another Action Man again and soon they all sat in front of the TV again as if nothing had happened.

Joe Hall (8)

The Haunted House

It was a very long time ago in Transylvania when some strange things happened. Two boys from Britain were on vacation in a house there.

'This is spookier than our attic,' said Peter as they saw a shadow moving past them in the darkness.

'What is it?' asked Sam.

They saw a huge figure moving slowly towards them.

'Vampire,' they both screamed.

The vampire hissed, 'I want blood.'

'Do you?' replied Peter bravely. 'Well, take light instead.'

'Argh!' The vampire melted.

Suddenly Frankenstein stood before them. He had a brain so he picked up the stake Sam put in the vampire's chest and started moving towards them.

'Now what are we going to do?' asked Sam.

'I know,' said Peter, 'take his brain out or electrocute him.'

'Electrocute him,' shouted Sam. 'Where are we going to get electricity?'

Peter tugged at Frankenstein's leg and said, 'Hey big brute, over here.'

Frankenstein followed him outside and got

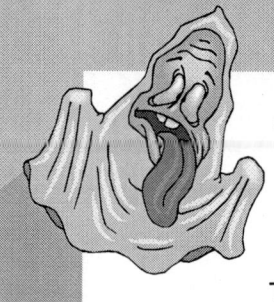

electrocuted by walking into the wires from the street light. He collapsed dead.

The boys went down into the cellar that looked like a dungeon. A gruesome, horrible ghost appeared. He was easy to deal with. They sprinkled some salt on him and he vanished.

Sam said, 'Let's get out of here. Our work is finished. It was fun but we have to go back now.'

He and Peter left to go to the airport to fly home.

Jack Cessford (9)

The Strange Ghost

George woke up in the middle of the night because he was having a bad dream. As he was trying to get back to sleep he suddenly noticed a transparent white shape.

He whispered, 'Hello,' because he was not sure it was real or if it was his imagination but a voice answered.

'Hello George.'

George asked, 'How do you know my name? Who are you and why are you here?'

The shape told George that its name was Fred and that he was a ghost who had lived in George's house a long, long time. He said that he liked children, especially babies. He asked George where the babies were and George remembered that his aunty had visited yesterday with her two terrible, noisy, six-month-old twins. He knew that he was supposed to visit his aunty tomorrow and asked Fred the ghost if he wanted to come.

George, his mam and Fred went to George's aunty's. The twins were crying. Fred went in and looked at them. They stopped crying straight away, in fact they started laughing. When George and his mam had to go, Fred stayed.

Each time George and his mam went to visit George's aunty and the babies George thought they looked more and more like ghosts and were behaving like ghosts too. His aunty and mam did not seem to notice so it was alright. George never had a bad dream again either.

Jonny Wilson (9)

The Ghost Wash

Kim and James were going on a trip. They were going together to Costa Bravo. They got out of school early so they could pack for the flight but they never knew that they would stay in a haunted hotel.

They landed right in front of the hotel they were staying in. Kim and James had a wonderful time swimming and playing in the sun.

Then, one night they were up late and they peeked through a door. They saw lots of people but they were really zombies. Kim screamed and some of the zombies stared at the children with glossy, dark, ghostly, hollow eyes. James noticed that they had no teeth but bright red holes for mouths. The children ran but some zombies came after them. James and Kim dived into the swimming pool. The zombies stopped and left. James had a plan. He got some buckets and filled then with water. Kim helped. Then they went back to where the zombies were and threw the water at them. The zombies melted away into the floor.

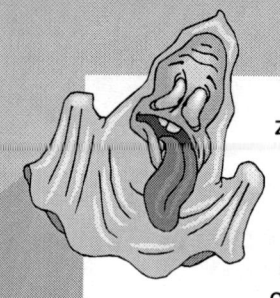

The next day the children went home. They had nightmares of ghosts touching them in bed for a while but were really glad to be back home. With a bit of luck the zombies would not come back to life again.

Jessica Rump (9)

Haunted House

There was a house. Not a normal house. It was a haunted house. It was at the very, very back of the rainforest. That's where it is cold and nobody ever went near there. Why? Because there had been some strange things happening, like the very foolish man who went in there and never came back out. Some say he had been killed. Nobody knew.

One day, a hunter who was shooting living things was trying to shoot a fox. It ran to the very back of the rainforest and so did the hunter. That's where the haunted house was. The fox slipped into the haunted house with the hunter close behind. They never came back out. Just like the very foolish man who never came back out. People said they died. Nobody knew.

A boy called Thomas heard about what was happening. He wanted to explore the haunted house, but he thought if he went in alone he would possibly not come back out. He asked his best friend Jack to come with him. They took armour from a castle, a torch because in a haunted house it would be dark and a hoover for protection. Now they would be able to find out what had created such a horrible mystery.

    They went in. They saw ghosts and sucked them all up into the hoover. The mystery was solved. The house was saved and Thomas and Jack now live at the very, very back of the rainforest.

Thomas Dingwall (9)

The Olympic Games

'Hey Tom, want to come and play in the garden?'

    'Nah Shannon, it's boring.'

    After dinner Shannon went on her own to play outside.

    Shannon soon went back inside. She walked slowly to her bedroom. Tom decided to follow. He heard Shannon crying. Tom ran to stay by her. Shannon squeezed Tom happily.

    Suddenly an extraordinary thing happened. A ghost popped up from nowhere. 'Hello,' said the ghost. 'Hey dudes, wanna practise for the Olympic games?'

    Shannon and Tom were surprised. Why would a ghost practise for the Olympic games? The ghost had shorts, running shoes, a baseball top and cap on.

    Shannon and Tom went outside with the ghost to practise for the Olympic games. They worked very hard.

    The next week the Olympic games were set up. Tom, Shannon and the ghost arrived. It was huge and everybody was watching them and the other contestants.

    The day began with Shannon's turn at running.

    '1, 2, 3, go!' shouted the man with the megaphone.

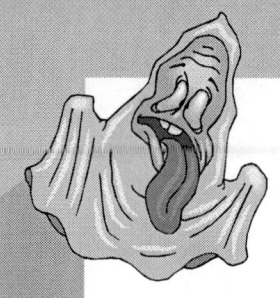

Shannon ran for her life until she was in last place. She eventually got to second at the end of the race.

'Here's your 2nd place ribbon,' said the man.

Shannon never realised that Tom joined the race and came last. He didn't get a ribbon. The ghost decided they should give up and they left.

At home they watched TV and the ghost disappeared. Suddenly, Shannon and Tom fell to the floor.

Dead!

The ghost stabbed them with an invisible knife. Second and last had not been good enough.

Iona Broomes (8)

The Haunted House

One terrible, snowy day, Britney and her mother, Clare, were coming home from the supermarket. It was about 6 o'clock in the evening. Just then they came to an old house and there was a clash.

This was bad. The car had broken down and it was right outside the house.

'Go on Britney, go and knock on the door. I'll be right there,' muttered Clare.

As Britney was about to knock she heard creaking noises and the door opened.

As Britney went in she saw nothing. It was an empty, derelict house. It looked like nobody had lived there for years. There were cobwebs and nails sticking up from the floorboards. Apart from that it looked pretty safe. Britney walked over the floorboards and all of a sudden there was a pat on her shoulder.

'Boo!'

She looked quickly behind her.

'Hi, I'm Casper, I'm a ghost.'

'Argh!' screamed Britney.

'I'm Casper.'

Britney was shocked. She asked Casper if she could have a phone to call a repair man. Just then she saw a brick fall down. She ran out and got in the car.

Britney's mother, Clare, looked at her and said, 'You look like you've seen a ghost.'

Hannah Bilton (9)

The Haunted Castle

Lucy and Erin were going on a school trip. They said bye to their mam and dad and got on the bus. After an hour they got off the bus and walked up the path to the castle.

Lucy and Erin were walking around and they ended up in front of the haunted castle. Erin was too scared to open the door so Lucy opened it. Then a sudden creaking noise came from inside the castle so they tiptoed into the castle. The door suddenly shut behind them. Erin was terrified, but Lucy kept on walking.

Soon a ghost came and stole Lucy.

Erin whispered, 'This is very scary isn't it L . . . Lucy?' She heard nothing. 'L . . . Lu . . . Lucy!' shouted Erin.

Soon she heard very strange noises. A

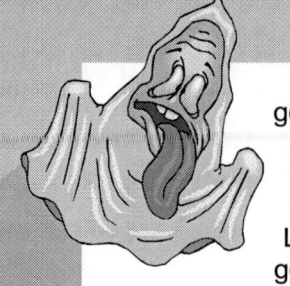

good ghost came and told Erin where Lucy was. The ghost said she was in the cupboard. Erin crept over to the cupboard and turned the handle slowly. Inside was Lucy. Erin pulled Lucy out of the cupboard. Then Lucy saw the good ghost in the hall. The good ghost warned them never to come in the castle again, so they opened the door and ran out of the castle and never came back again. Then they saw their classmates outside the castle and ran over to them.

Helen Burns (9)

There's Something In The Basement

Jim and his mam and dad moved into a mansion. It was all dark and spooky. The next day he went to school and told his friends about his new home. They said a boy from school went in and never came out. This made Jim afraid, although his mum and dad said it was nonsense.

The next night he heard some footsteps and decided to investigate. He went down into the basement and he heard more noises. Suddenly something tapped him on the shoulder and he rushed out but his mum and dad didn't believe him.

He went to school the next morning and he didn't say a word about last night even though people asked him. When it was time for bed that night he decided to put a stop to it. *I'm getting that ghost out,* he thought.

The next night he heard the noises and went down again. He saw the ghost and said, 'Why are you making noises?'

The ghost nearly jumped on him.

'I'm not scared of you,' said Jim.

The ghost was never seen again.

Emily Winlow (8)

The Jellyfish Beach Ghost

127 years ago, aboard The Sea Lion, Howard and Jack were searching for treasure. They found it. Then Howard, who was greedy, wanted it all to himself, so he stabbed Jack twice and threw him in the sea.

Underneath the murky waters, a giant jellyfish immediately attacked him and sucked him dry of fluids. Jack came back as a giant jellyfish for revenge.

Sarah Deslate was lying on the beach reading an interesting book. She decided to take a dip in the sea - the water was warm.

Sarah wanted to stay late, make a fire and roast marshmallows. She made up her mind to take one last swim before starting the fire so she gingerly edged her way into the water. The last rays of the sun were dissolving into the sea, making Sarah feel as though she were bathing in blood. She'd swum out a few metres when something tugged at her foot. She thought she had just got her foot tangled in some algae so she tried to untangle herself, but the thing tugging her foot was resistant. Slowly she was sinking into the watery unknown. she didn't even have time to scream.

Early the next morning, the police conducted a search. They found Sarah's fluidless body bobbing out to sea.

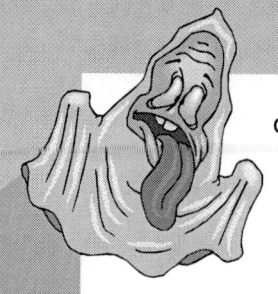

Jack the jellyfish wanted revenge on only one person so the murders ceased.

Luiza Deaconescu (12)

The Broomly Ghost

John and David went on a school trip to a mansion at Bromley Grange with three teachers. While they were there they did lots of exciting things.

On the first night at the mansion, John and David decided to explore.

'Come on John,' shouted David. 'I want to go and explore.'

They started to walk down the stairs and made their way through a maze of intertwining old rooms. They took their torches so that they could see as the lights had been turned off. When they turned the corner of the last room they heard a floorboard creaking in the distance. John turned quickly and shone the torch to see if anything was there.

'I can't see anything,' John whispered.

'Let's keep on going,' David replied.

As they made their way into the dark and gloomy courtyard, the heavy wooden door slammed behind them causing both of them to jump up in fright.

'Let's get out of here,' cried John.

They scrambled through the back door so that they would not wake their teachers. When they got back into their room both of them went straight to sleep.

The following night, John and David decided to have one last look around the mansion before they went home.

They decided to explore the attic. The attic was boring, full of dusty boxes and mice droppings.

Suddenly a dark shadow appeared from the far, cobweb-filled corner. The boys went a deathly white and ran screaming back to their room once more.

To this day the boys have never told a soul about the spooky happenings in the mansion.

Fay Stafford (12)

Victorian Ghost

We got out of the taxi and we entered the Ritz Hotel. We went up the golden stairs. I felt a shiver up my spine, but kept walking.

One night I saw things move so I crept over to my mam and told her everything.

'Don't be silly,' she said.

I heard talking but I thought it was my parents.

Morning came and we went shopping. In the afternoon I asked if I could have a sandwich. Room service came and I got tingles. When the person left I saw a small brown letter saying, 'Bring a wooden musical jewellery box to the courtyard'.

At 9 o'clock I went to bed.

At midnight I was woken by a sound. I followed the sound and reached a door. Suddenly it stopped.

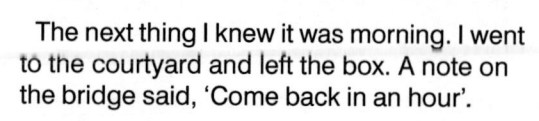

The next thing I knew it was morning. I went to the courtyard and left the box. A note on the bridge said, 'Come back in an hour'.

When I came back there was nothing there. When I left I had the urge to go back. There was a gold necklace with 'Emily' written on it. I wondered how it knew my name. There was a letter nearby saying, 'I have gone, but you are the only one that can get this necklace. Hear me'.

Suddenly I heard 'Hello?'

I went back and I wrote a letter saying thank you. I went back and left it and it suddenly disappeared. I walked away smiling.

Emily Burnett

Who Is It?

Last Sunday morning I went to visit my grandma in Crosshatch Hospital. I haven't been to this hospital before. Anyway, as I went through the wide open doors into the hospital I saw my grandma out of bed. I shouted, 'Grandma, what are you doing out of bed? You're supposed to be resting!' She's never usually out of bed.

She didn't reply.

I called again, 'Grandma!'

She replied this time, 'Yes dear?' she called.

She didn't sound like my grandma at all, in fact she wasn't my grandma.

She then took my hand and led me to a

dark room.

'How are you my dear? It's been a while,' she whispered. 'It's time you go to the stairs and see him,' she exclaimed.

I asked her, 'Who?'

She replied, 'Him at number 38 Costal Park Avenue, *go there now!*'

As I left the hospital after seeing my grandma, I thought about the lady in the hospital and what she had said to me. As I walked through Coastal Park Avenue I walked into the house as the lady had given me a key.

When I stepped into the house I saw some dark stairs like the lady had mentioned to me. As I climbed up the stairs I heard a noise, a strange noise, it was as if someone was there. When I reached the top, the light was shining through the window, then there he was - floating in the light shining through the window. It's him, it's him.

Nichola Mason (12)

The Note

It was one sunny day. I was at my cousin's house. I was with my friend called Jenny. The house was very big and was called Middlethorp Manor. I had had some very disturbing nightmares about this house.

Jenny and I decided to have a wander around the house through all the doors and rooms. We went up the stairs but the thing was each time we were going to enter another room we felt as though there was someone lurking in the room.

We walked up the stairs and then there was another little second set of stairs which we went up. This was about 4-5 steps. We both got a chill down our spine each time we went up these stairs. We got scared, screamed and ran down both sets of stairs.

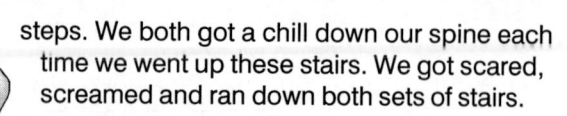

A half an hour later we went into the garden and on the climbing frame. We were sitting on a swing each and we both had this feeling that somebody was in the farmer's field behind us. We ran straight back inside.

Next we found what was called a pulley, it went from downstairs to upstairs. We put nothing in it and ran straight upstairs and opened the door but there was a note on the shelf and it said, well we couldn't really read what it said so we went downstairs and showed it to my mam and she read . . . 'We are watching you'.

Abigail Bowmaker (12)

Adventure Accident

Me and my friends were fifteen when we went on holiday. We planned to have an adventure weekend in France, staying in tents, enjoying the scenery and fishing in the river next to our field.

What more could we ask for than spectacular weather and peace and quiet?

However, after looking around the area we noticed a huge cottage and we later found out that a couple called Mr and Mrs Costa lived there with their daughter, Ezra, who sleep-walked.

Every night Ezra's parents had to lock all of the doors in the house. But a tragic event happened one night after Ezra's parents had celebrated and had a party at the local pub they were rather drunk and they forgot to lock the doors, unsurprisingly Ezra escaped and we later found out that she had drowned in the river where we went fishing every morning. When Dylan found her dead body he screamed and cried.

She was very stiff and her eyes were red and open, she also now had no eyelashes. Her skin was white and pale.

We were all physically sick as we saw insects feasting on her wet hair.

The next morning Ezra Costa was announced dead.

The village is now completely empty and her poor body is buried in her old back garden.

I believe that her ghost haunts the village today.

Everybody wonders whatever happened to Mr and Mrs Costa and their belongings.

Emma Winter (12)

A Walk To Remember

It was the night before Hallowe'en and all the shop shelves were covered in scary and horrifying decorations. The staff were all in costumes such as goblins and witches, but one person stood out!

It was a man dressed up as Frankenstein with the scarred face and the nails coming out of his head. The only strange thing was that he did not look like he was in costume and when you looked into his eyes they were the same colour as his skin. I looked down at my watch, I saw that the time was eight and I was to be home at nine. It took about half an hour to walk home. The staff were trying to get people out of the shop, I was the last person to get out. The shutters shut and the lights went off and I started my journey home in the pitch-black of the night. As I took my first step . . .

I walked along a narrow path with grass either side with the trees weeping over. I met an old lady walking towards me.

She said, 'Don't go on, turn around!'

I said, 'Why?'

I kept on walking to then come across a dead end and decomposed man with a colony of flies buzzing around him! I felt sick!

As I walked home I could not get it out of my head, it was like a parasite, it would not go away. I then heard a noise, *crash, bang!*

Paul Rooney (13)

Silence

I was sitting at home on a hot summer's day when my phone rang. It was Verity's mum. She told me that Verity was really ill and wouldn't talk anymore! I went to their three-floored mansion straight away. Verity was looking pale and lifeless. She didn't say a word till her mum left the room, then slowly told me that she'd seen it.

'Seen what?' I questioned, but to that I got no answer.

She also asked me to go to the attic and get her teddy, I couldn't understand why she wanted him as she put him in the attic two years ago! I decided not to question her will and left the room wondering why she wanted Alfie.

As I walked past her parents' room I caught sight of the newly polished banister. I began to wonder what Verity had seen. I squeezed the banister tightly and walked up the first flight of stairs with great care and tried to be as silent as possible. As I approached the second flight of stairs there was a noticeable drop in temperature I couldn't understand as it was warm up to the second flight of stairs! I decided to run up the second flight of stairs as it sent chills up my spine. I got to the third flight and the temperature was still low, it felt like something was following me, so I dashed in the attic and looked for Alfie. Just as I found him I heard giggling from behind. I slowly turned around and at that moment I knew exactly what Verity had seen earlier . . .

Isra Gabal (13)

Flash/Bang

I was at a friend's house, it was a modern, cosy house, rather large for my liking though. The carpets were clean, the furniture was polished and the expensive pictures on the wall were perfectly centred on the magnolia-coloured walls, which gave a warm, friendly, welcoming feeling.

The night had passed and morning was calling. We had been up all night watching scary movies so I was rather uncomfortable with flashbacks of the movies going through my head. I felt the need to freshen myself up, so I went to ask for directions to the bathroom, when I realised everyone was fast asleep. Anyway I decided to have a wander. I found myself in a dark room filled with sparkling ornaments.

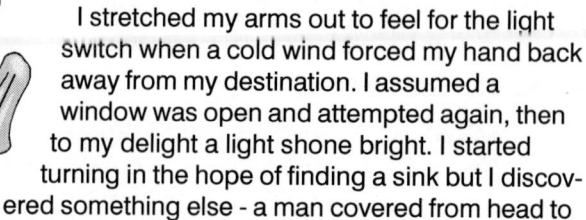

I stretched my arms out to feel for the light switch when a cold wind forced my hand back away from my destination. I assumed a window was open and attempted again, then to my delight a light shone bright. I started turning in the hope of finding a sink but I discovered something else - a man covered from head to toe in dark clothing who was standing with a lightning bolt in his scarred hands.

Suddenly I saw a flash, a huge firing lightning bolt was heading in my direction. It was happening in slow motion until the bang, the bellowing of the thunder belting against the window. After that, well, let's just say I never saw one more movie and neither did my friend.

Bethany Hammonds (13)

Eleven-Foot Door

All was dark, the house seemed empty. A light flicked on. It was the highest window in the tall, and what looked like, historical building that lit up. So there was actually someone in, what looked like, the suspended building. Did someone or something occupy the building? That was the question that was rushing through my brain . . . the building just looked as if there was something bad waiting to happen in it.

I decided to knock on the door because I really needed to ring home. I wouldn't normally have decided on this house to use a telephone but it was my only choice out in the country after my car had broken down. I knocked on the what must have been eleven-foot door. No answer. Just as I turned to walk away I heard a loud creaking noise, the door was opening very, very slowly. I took it as if that whoever was opening the door was having trouble opening it, so I started to help open the door. It was extremely heavy. Eventually we/I got it open . . . I wasn't sure what was on the other side of the door, I walked in and shouted, 'Hello?' There was no answer again. I walked two steps further into this massive hallway. I heard a loud squeaking noise coming from the top of the stairs. I went up to inspect because I thought someone was hurt and that was the mistake I made . . . there it was, one metre in front of me . . .

Andrew McCarrick (13)

Hallowe'en Horror

It was a Hallowe'en night and me and my friends go trick or treating every year. I was so excited. I bought my outfit from my favourite Hallowe'en shop, 'Spooked Silly'. My new outfit was a scary witch. I put facepaints on and false nails. My mum said I looked really scary. So me, Vicky, Sarah, John and Jack went to trick or treat.

Every year we go to a spectacular house, the owners invite one person only in to get a treat and it was my turn to go to this house. I thought they were jealous, so I dragged them along.

It was a wonderful house, very light and clean. They took me upstairs and into a room where they kept their baby boy. I asked when I could have my present. The baby started to cry. I looked at him and they said I could kiss him, so I did on the cheek. I suddenly felt cold. My teeth were growing. I turned around and saw what my friends didn't want to come here for, I knew now that I shouldn't have come.

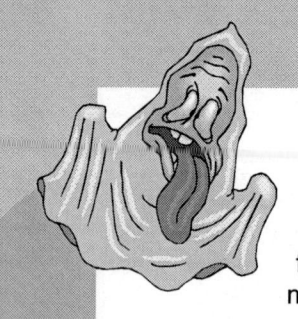

I tried to run but I couldn't, then it struck me that I couldn't move at all. I could hear laughing getting fainter and fainter. I fell to the ground. What was happening? My hands, my face, my feet were changing. I looked in a mirror. No, *no! Help . . . !*

Laurie Slesser (13)

The Voices

I had just watched a scary film on TV. No one else was in the house. I was alone. Then the phone rang. I was scared to answer it, but I did.

'Hello?' I said. My voice was trembling.

There were voices echoing, 'Don't go!'

'Don't go!'

'Don't go!'

'June 13th!'

I screamed and slammed the phone down. I ran around the house locking every window and door. Then the phone rang again. I picked it up. 'What do you want?' I shouted as my voice shook with horror!

'Amy? What's wrong?' Sammy shouted with fright.

'Oh hi Sammy, I'm OK, you just scared me!'

'Do you want to come to the cinema on the bus with me next week?'

I looked at my diary, Saturday 13th June was the day she invited me, then I remembered the voices had said 'Don't go!'.

'I'm sorry, I'm babysitting that night,' I said, feeling guilty.

'It's OK, I will invite Mandy!' Amy exclaimed.

'OK, bye!' I put the phone down and forgot about the voices.

A week later, the day after Saturday 13th June, I was flicking through the channels on the TV and all of a sudden I saw on the news that a bus had crashed on Saturday 13th June and a girl had been killed - the reporter said Mandy Hulme - *I screamed!*

That could have been me that died! I would have been on that bus with Sammy! I remembered the voices told me 'Don't go!' but who were they?

Daniella Dunning (13)

The Curse Of 666

It was a dark, stormy night that night and I remember it all so well, the house and all the things that happened. It started when me, Josh and Dan all dared each other to go into the house, the haunted house. That night we snuck out and went on our way to the house. When we reached the tall, black gates I wished I had never agreed to come.

We pushed open the gate and walked to the big wooden door. As we pushed open the door the smell of rotten flesh blew at me like a gust of wind. Suddenly lightning flashed and we saw hundreds of dead people nailed to upside down crosses and 666 carved into their bodies. I looked behind to where Dan was. Lightning flashed and I saw Dan was nailed to a cross with 666 on his forehead. Me and Josh ran home as fast as our legs would carry us. I reached home and wondered where Josh was. That was it, I never saw them again.

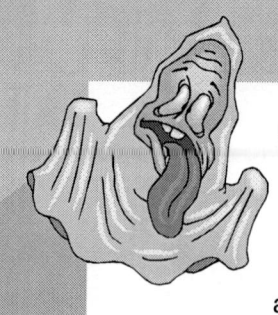

The next morning there was a gravestone in my room with my name on it. The year I was born and the year I died. I turned to the mirror and 666 was on my forehead.

Thomas Williamson (12)

Face Your Fear!

Elizabeth slept peacefully. She got up and walked downstairs. Not disturbing anyone, she got to the front door. Quietly she slid out.

She walked down the cold and lonely street and came to the graveyard. She walked through the gates and they slammed shut behind her. Elizabeth walked past the graves and then came to a newly dug grave.

A gust of wind flew at her and wrapped round Elizabeth. It carried her to some steps. Elizabeth walked down the steps, she came to a room. It was pitch-black. Then a match struck and a man's voice spoke out loud.

'Hello Elizabeth, it's your special day today.'

He took her to the grave that had been made. On it was written the name 'Elizabeth Sky' and 'Died on November 13th'. This was today's date but Elizabeth didn't know it yet.

'Elizabeth, you will face your fear today,' said the strange man.

He threw her down, she landed and awoke.

She looked around and screamed, she had been sleep-walking and now she had to pay the price for walking into danger.

'Who are you?' screamed the terrified girl.

'I am the ghost of fear, to show you to your death,' replied the ghoulish voice.

A few minutes went by and Elizabeth passed out. She woke up and reached her hands out, she couldn't, she couldn't even move. Then she realised that she had been buried, buried alive. Her greatest fear had become a reality.

Alicia McCluckie (12)

Gory Story

It was the 31st of October when it all happened, the 'it' I'm referring to is the unlucky kidnapping where me and my friend got abducted by three men in a Nissan Skyline, or it might have been a Mitsubishi Lancer, I forget, it is all quite blurred.

They pulled up and called over, 'So you want some food?'

David, my mate, ran over. He put one sweet in his mouth and keeled over. I turned round and ran but I felt a sharp pain between my shoulders and my world turned into technicoloured bubbles.

I woke up two hours later, tied and gagged in the boot of the car, but David wasn't there. I called out and they opened the boot but all that came out was a muffled sound past the gag, but they heard all the same. They took the gag off, and I said, 'Where is David?' Apparently he died before he recovered.

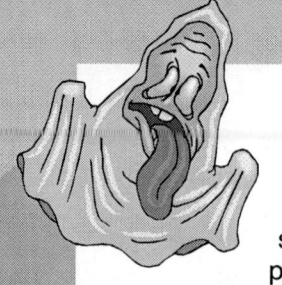

Suddenly a scream erupted from the wall and a white shape came flying through the wall and away again. I had soiled myself by then and so had the men. I think the next second it happened again, but this time it passed through one of the men and he collapsed dead on the floor.

'What the . . . ?' but it happened again.

This time it stopped and said, 'Let him go,' and killed another one of the men. One left now. It came in for the last time, so there it ended, and I'm here now.

Josh Palmer (13)

The Night On Christmas Day

When I was little, about 5 years ago, I can remember a really freaky story. It happened at my best friend's house. She lived just down the street. It happened like this.

I was walking down the street until I came to Sara's house. Down the garden path, past the bright yellow sunflowers until I reached the big white door with the bright gold letter box. Sara answered and let me in.

As I walked in I could feel the hot air pushing past me as if I was walking through a desert. As we went upstairs into Sara's room I felt the temperature go right up. I was wondering how Sara didn't look bothered or interested. As I walked into Sara's room all that I could see was purple.

There was purple everywhere, carpet,

curtains, wallpaper etc. But one thing that spooked me out was in one of the corners of her room was a big crack and I could feel cold air from outside pushing past my finger. Sara didn't notice it until I had told her. There was a secret that Sara had never told me about. I asked her if she would tell me but all she'd said was it was about her house.

I started to hear noises, I thought it was nothing at first. After a while the same noise started getting louder. I started to shake very slowly. I turned round to look at Sara, she stared back and I think this was her secret . . .

Amanda Currey (12)

Scream

That scream, the blood-curdling scream kept me awake at night. I wondered what it was that had made such a frightful noise. I wondered whether I should have gone and helped the person or was it a person? Could a person make such a noise? A person or not that scream haunted me in my sleep. I wasn't sure what happened that night but I just remembered walking down the dark alleyway and feeling that somebody was following me. I remember cautiously turning around and seeing nothing but darkness. I knew I should have taken the long route where there were people about but instead I took the dangerous path that led me straight to the scream. I didn't turn around after that, I just concentrated on walking.

My pace got faster but so did the person's behind me. I began to run: I just kept getting faster and faster until . . . there was a loud high-pitched scream coming from the wood behind me. I froze. I carefully turned around and saw smoke wafting into the air behind me. I was scared to move but the thought of staying around made my heart pound with worry.

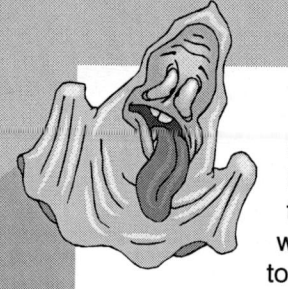

I ran home as fast as I could and collapsed onto my bed. I didn't tell a soul about what had happened because I didn't want anyone to know that I'd left somebody to possibly die when maybe I could have helped. The guilt was too much for me to handle, I just wanted to forget.

Charlotte Lynch

Haunting Elizabeth

In a school in London, there were two friends called Lauren and Carly. Their worst lesson was with Miss Ward, which was history.

They came in as usual. Miss Ward explained what they had to do. They looked through a history book and saw a picture of a young girl called Elizabeth.

The bell rang so Lauren and Carly packed up their things and left. They were talking about Elizabeth whilst scaring themselves, when Carly needed the toilet.

They both went in a cubicle, when Lauren finished she pulled the chain. Carly bent down to do up her shoe laces. As she looked up she saw familiar black boots. Elizabeth was hanging with a knife in her hand, staring at Carly.

Carly screamed as loud as she could. Lauren ran up to her and asked what was wrong. Carly was just pointing into the cubicle.

Lauren could see how freaked out Carly was so she offered to sleep round her house, because her parents were away, so they went to Carly's house.

The phone rang, it was a prank.

Lauren got scared and decided to go home. She was halfway up the road when she realised she had left her bag.

Lauren walked into Carly's house and into her bedroom. She found Carly hanging over her bed with a knife through her hand. She was staring at Lauren.

Was Carly Elizabeth or did Elizabeth come and kill Carly?

No one knows!

Lauren Henden (13)

Insomnia Kills

I tried to sleep, but as usual I couldn't, ever since Dad died . . . something told me I wasn't safe, somehow I felt I wasn't alone.

I lifted my duvet; the cold wind coming from the open window sent a chill down my spine. I put my legs off the bed, slowly I got out of bed and stood up, and I reached towards the window.

I heard a bang . . . I looked outside and saw something . . . lingering in the bushes, a figure of some sort . . . I quickly pulled the windows . . . they wouldn't close! It felt as if they were stuck . . . I stepped back . . . something was wrong . . .

Suddenly something pushed me onto the bed, something pushed down on my ribs, I couldn't breathe . . . I couldn't see . . . it started to get colder, the force had stopped . . .

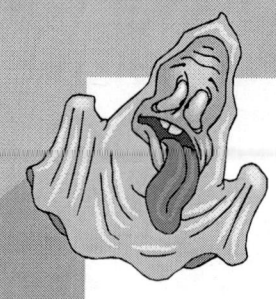

Desperately gasping for air I struggled to move back, I still couldn't see anything, I heard snarling . . .

'Go . . . go . . . go!' said a voice I recognised.

Something started pulling me towards the window, pulling me like a magnet . . . the force was too strong . . . I couldn't fight it . . . I couldn't breathe . . .

Suddenly I was flung out of the window, I had landed on the top of the gate . . . the rusty, sharp spike had gone right through me, my head and legs were dangling, lifeless, paralysed, painful . . . I had no energy left . . . it had got me . . . I recognised it . . . it was . . .

'Daddy?'

The creature nodded.

Shazia Hussain (14)

Boy From Beyond

'Hannah . . . Hannah!'

Hannah woke up with a start, sitting bolt upright, screaming so much it felt as if her lungs were about to burst.

The bedroom door swung open as her mother sprang into the room. She rushed to her side, placing her hand on her daughter's slippery forehead. She took it away, engulfed in sweat.

'What's wrong sweetie?' she asked, attempting to remain calm.

Hannah broke off her scream and swallowed hard.

'There's a boy, there!' she exclaimed, pointing to a dark shadowy corner of the room, 'Can't you see him? He knows my name!'

Her mother spun round, staring edgily into the scene her daughter had pointed out, but saw nothing. Her heart leaping in her chest, she took Hannah in her arms and exited the room, slamming the door forcefully behind her.

'There's definitely something in that room, but I can't see it,' Hannah's mother reasoned down the phone to her friend Janet.

'Well, my watch stops every time I go in there, and Luke's a total sceptic and he swore he heard a boy calling his name,' her friend replied.

The cold, ghostly sightings occurred more frequently. The boy, showing half of his pale face only to Hannah, the rest submerged in darkness, whispering softly, yet piercing the night's silence.

Hannah was soundly sleeping, sharing a large room with her two sisters, Amber and Jade. The boy still stands absent-mindedly, waiting for the abandoned room's next resident.

Kerry Brown (12)

It's All Just Black And White

James ran as fast as he could, the door looming ahead of him. He could hear the shouts of his pursuers who were right on his tail. He knew he could do it, he had to do it. The door opened as if greeting his limp, slack jawed, muddy body. A throng of people swarmed towards him and he lost all sight of his goal. People shouted as he barged his way through.

He grabbed hold of the door and forced himself past everyone else. *I have made it*, he thought to himself. Just round the corner was the one room that he knew was safe.

Then she was there; his fear came flooding back. Her pearly-white figure looming over him. He spun on the spot and ran smack-bang into the most ugly creature you have ever seen. It was the opposite of the ghost behind, it was a short, stumpy figure with a charcoal-black face. It seemed, if possible, to consist of darkness. Only the marble-white of its flowing hair seemed to be free from the spell that kept him there, the spell that prevented him from being rotten and dead. Instead a blackened corpse dressed in rags hung like a puppet in front of James. He wanted to scream, but he couldn't muster the breath nor the will to do so. He knew that this was the end, for all of mankind! He could do nothing at all for them now . . .

Anthony Williams (14)

Exorcism

The room was dark, a family sat in the corner shivering, and pointing behind the man. The man's gaze went from the tip of the shaking finger to the boy behind him, his breath coming out as clouds before him. The boy looked different, his eyes distant, mouth open, complexion grey. Yellow teeth protruded from cracked, blue lips. Blood leaked from between those teeth, and leaked down over the head, thick, purple blood seeping from the gaping hole where the crown once was.

A hammer in his hand, the boy advanced, right into the man's outstretched hand . . . a hand containing a cross. *'May the power of Christ compel ye!'* With every shout the boy faded, advancing ever closer, the blood erupting from his skull, a dull, deep howl echoed around the room, blood sprayed from his mouth, dripping from the walls.

'May . . . the . . . power . . . of . . . Christ . . . compel . . . ye!' He gasped the last word as the boy faded out of sight and the lights flickered on. The man wiped his face with a hanky, got up and left the house. He reached out with his hand and the coat flew through the door to his hand. He faced away from the house and made his way over the horizon.

Simon Jeffries (16)

The Gomms

There is a very abnormal family - the Gomms. The children never attended school, the parents were unemployed. They live in a castle, up high on a big hill. No one goes up there - too scared. The children are Harriet and Louie. The parents are Elizabeth and Frankie.

It's weird, the family's name has appeared in books for centuries, their house is said to be haunted, everything within that castle is dead. Everyone's a bit spooked out.

I decided to keep a watch on the castle. So I stayed up. There was a storm. I looked up out of my window into the sky. It was a full moon. *Werewolves!* No! I stared at the castle, my eyes falling out of their sockets in amazement. There were white spirits floating through the windows. I was about to scream. It was them alright, I recognised the children at once. Harriet's long blonde hair, Louie's curly brown. The stories were true.

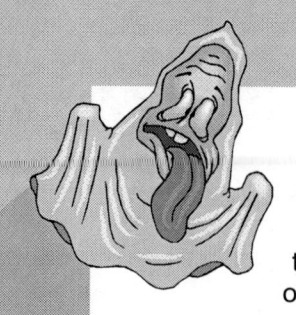

I trembled as I reached in my cupboard to grab my camera. It was loaded, I focused the 'target' on the ghosts now starting to muff out the light so they were unseen. I clicked and took the picture twice in case it didn't come out.

I crept back to bed. I suddenly heard a rattling at my window. The thunder and lightning crashed. Standing at my window was Louie. Grinning his head off, literally his head fell to the floor. Harriet cackled. Thank goodness it was a dream. No ghosts!

Samantha Gibbons (13)

Spook Town Graveyard

One day I was walking in the park next to the graveyard and I felt a shiver down my spine so I thought, *don't worry, it's only the wind*, until I heard a voice say my name and that's when I really started to get the creeps. Then I started to think there were people all around me under the ground! Then after that I ran straight back home, I had had enough of being freaked out for one day.

Then a week later once again I heard the ghosts of Spook Town graveyard calling my name and it was as if they were dragging me by some magic force to the gravedigger's shed and then before I knew it, I was in front of it. My body was shaking like jelly, my heart was beating ten to the dozen and then the doors swung open in front of my very own eyes and there he was, the gravedigger of Spook Town graveyard who nobody had seen for fifty whole years. He went missing in 1946.

Hhe said to me in a very spooky and deep crackly voice, 'You have disturbed the ghosts of Spook Town graveyard and now you must pay!'

I was sweating and my heart was beating faster than ever before, things were going through my head, *what do I do? How do I get out?* Then all at once I heard my mum shouting my name.

'Sean! Sean!'

Then I woke up and sweat was dropping from my face. Thank God, it was all a nightmare.

Sean Jones (12)

Horror House!

The sun shining, birds singing: a beautiful day, but it was about to change!

We had arrived at our new house; Dad was moving furniture into my bedroom.

'Sarah, can you cook dinner? Dad and I are going out,' said Mum.

'OK, bye.'

I looked at the house, a chill ran down my spine. I ran to my bedroom. A young boy stood in front of me staring coldly. I froze.

'Why are you in my house?' he said in a mournful voice.

'I'm sorry, this is my house,' I shouted.

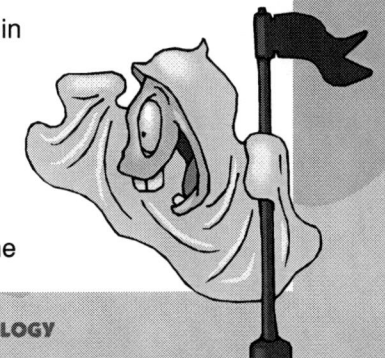

Gasping with fright I noticed blood oozing from the walls; dead people appeared as though suspended from the ceiling. I screamed with terror and ran down the stairs, the boy following. He grabbed me and forced me into the basement. He tore at the basement wall. Again I screamed, so terrified I couldn't breathe. There was a dead body behind the wall. This was no ordinary boy! It was his rotting body in the wall. He hurled me into the broken wall, and completely sealed it up. Struggling to breathe, I choked and blacked out . . .

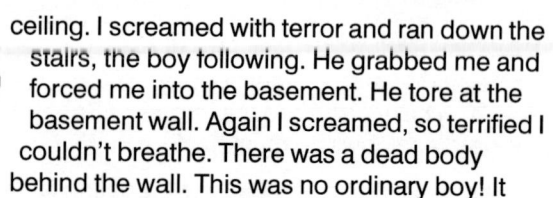

My parents blamed themselves for my disappearance, the police never did find me.

Two months later my parents moved out. There were too many memories for them to bear. We watched, the boy and I, as my parents left and after a last glance we walked away from my bedroom window.

So here we are, in Horror House, waiting for our next victim.

Keeley Knight (12)

The Haunted House

It was one Friday afternoon when Louise and big sister Jo got home from a very hectic day at school, when they found out that they were going to move house on that weekend. They were very surprised because they loved their house. They had no choice because their parents found a job there.

'We do not want to leave the school we are going to because we have all of our friends there and we don't want to leave them all behind,' said Jo to her mum and dad.

'We can't stay because we need the money for the bills and all the food for the house, sorry,' said Mum.

So that day they got their things sorted and boxed up ready to move out on Saturday. Louise had just finished packing her things when a letter came through the door addressed to her. She picked it up wondering who would send a letter to her. She opened and read it.

It said . . .

'Dear Louise,

I am writing to warn you that the lovely, beautiful, big house you are going to move into isn't that lovely as you think. It is haunted! Years ago a family lived there and they were all murdered, it is said that their spirits still fly around the house scaring the people that live there to move out.

Good luck.

?'

Louise took no notice of the letter and threw it into the bin, she then went to bed.

The next morning everyone was up bright and early at 7am, ready for the big move. It was now 2.45pm and they had packed all their things onto the two trucks. It was an hour drive there and it was so boring for Louise and Jo as they had nothing to do because their Game Boys and things like that were in the boxes and they couldn't get to them.

They were finally there and Jo and Louise decided to explore. They found nothing interesting, only a few cupboards that were left. They had then been called by their parents to come and help to unload the boxes from the trucks.

'Can't you and Dad unload the trucks, 'cause

A YOUNG WRITERS ANTHOLOGY

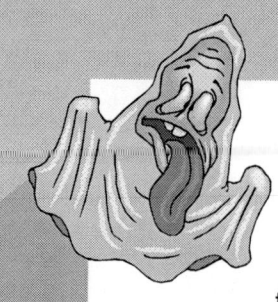

we are looking around the house at the moment?' Jo called down.

'No way, all the things aren't just mine and your dad's, they are yours and Louise's as well, so come down right now and get your things into your own rooms,' said their mum.

So they both came down and took their own things to their rooms, as quickly as they could. To them it took forever and they kept on moaning and moaning. Shortly after that it was time for dinner and the day had gone really quickly for everyone.

A few weeks after that it was the first day of a new school for Louise and Jo, they really didn't want to go because they didn't have any friends there. It was now time for the first lesson and lucky for Louise she had met a girl in her form who was in every lesson with her, her name was Hannah. So they both went round together all day long and Louise met some of Hannah's other good friends. They all got on very well. Jo had also made some friends that she had been hanging around with.

At the end of the day as Jo and Louise were walking home they didn't stop talking. They had so much to talk about and most of the way home they were both describing their new friends to each other. They both liked the sound of each other's friends and really wanted to meet them. When they got home there was a letter on the floor addressed to Louise.

She picked it up and read it, it said . . .

'Dear Louise,

I really tried to warn you and now you have moved there, it will not be long until the terrible spirits will scare you out of your house and if you don't go then I don't know what they will do to you. I did warn you.

?'

Louise didn't know what to do but keep the letter in her room. Later that night after they had all gone to bed, Louise needed her door open because she didn't like the dark that much. All of a sudden her door slammed shut and it was pitch-black, she decided to get up, turn the light on and open the door again. So she did but her light had stopped working and now Louise was getting really scared. She called for her mum and dad and they both came running in thinking it was an emergency, well it was for Louise.

'What is it darling?' said Dad.

'My door has just slammed shut and my light has stopped working,' Louise said really quickly, as she was panicking.

Her mum then flicked the light on and then off again. 'It does work Louise and the wind has probably made your door slam, so don't get so worried,' said Mum.

They went back to bed and left the door ajar, they also left Louise lying in bed wondering if the mysterious person who kept on writing to her was telling the truth. She really didn't know.

The next morning, when Louise and Jo were eating their breakfast, Jo kept on asking her what happened last night and didn't talk about anything else.

In form Louse was telling Hannah about the two letters and about what happened the night before. Hannah thought that she was only joking about, but that night when Hannah came round to sleep, she saw the letters and saw something quite strange happen.

Hannah got a little bit scared by this but she

A YOUNG WRITERS ANTHOLOGY

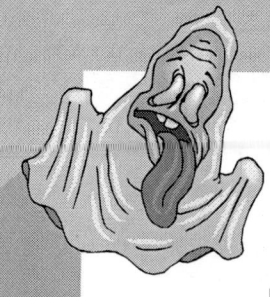

didn't let it ruin the good night that they were having together.

The next morning Hannah called home to see if she could stay until Sunday instead of going home on Saturday because Louise's mum said she could if it was alright with her mum.

'Louise, my mum said that I could and that she will be round in half an hour to take us to my house to give your mum and dad a break. So tell your parents that we will be home in time for dinner,' Hannah said to Louise.

'OK and I will bring a few things around as well,' Louise replied.

A few weeks on the spirits were scaring everyone even more, but Mum and Dad didn't think anything of it. Louise and Jo were getting really frightened and didn't like the house anymore. Their friends didn't want to go round their house anymore because they were getting really scared. They both tried to warn their parents but they didn't listen to them, they thought they were being silly.

About a year later something really terrible happened. Louise had found Jo dead on the sofa watching TV. It was said that she had been murdered by someone or something, nobody knows.

A day later Louise got another letter, it said…

'Louise, I am really sorry about your sister and I wish I could do something to help but I really can't. I think I know what killed her, it was the spirits and they will kill again if you don't leave. There is no way you and your family will survive if you don't move out now!

Best wishes, Luke.'

Louise knew who Luke was, he was her old school teacher who was always willing to help. But she couldn't understand how he of all people could know exactly where she had moved to. Again she decided to keep the letter in her room with the other ones that he'd sent to her a year ago.

The week after Louise had to go back to school, all of her friends were asking her if she knew how Jo had been killed.

'No, I don't know but I think I know what. I think it was those terrible spirits in the house but I am not that sure. Oh by the way, I have got another letter and I now know who is writing to me, it is Luke. Luke is my old school teacher but the weird thing is how he could know where I live now?' Louise said, feeling freaked out by the letter from Luke.

'You should be asking one of your closest friends back in your old school, they will probably know,' Hannah replied.

So that night Louise was looking everywhere to find the numbers of all her old school friends. Finally she found them and called all of them, but lucky for Louise the last person she called up knew.

She said, 'Sorry I told Luke where you were moving to and he thought that he would check it out on the Internet, but he never told me what was said about it.'

Louise was so relieved that she had now found out that Shelly had told Luke where she had moved to. But why? Louise could never understand why Shelly would tell Luke where she lived now, anyway they weren't that close.

A month later she had got another letter from Luke.

A YOUNG WRITERS ANTHOLOGY

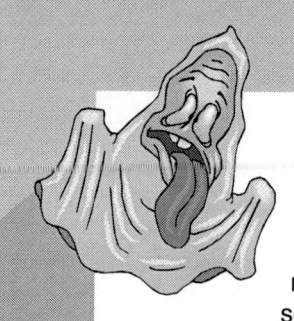

'Dear Louise,

All this information about your house was given to me off of the Internet and they are not lying, I know it. I really wish I could make it much easier for you but all I can do is keep sending you letters.

Love from Luke.'

This time Louise decided to send a reply letter to him. It said . . .

'Dear Luke,

Thank you for all of the letters, some of them have made me feel better and some of them have really scared me. But then again I wouldn't believe what the Internet tells you because they might be lying to you, you never know.

Thanks, Louise.'

This was sent to Luke the next day and it was a week until she had heard from him, but this time he called her. He said, 'Hello Louise, how are you?'

'I am fine, how are you?' Louise replied.

'I am fine. Well the reason I called you was to say thank you for the letter and to say that why on earth would I lie to you like that? Got to go, bye,' he said, then he just hung up.

Another month later Louise and her parents went to find a house, but not far away from their new school that they were in at the moment. It was a month until they moved and Louise was happy to leave the

house and to have her friends over now and again. She was happy to tell Luke that they had moved and he was happy to hear the good news.

After a while the haunted house was knocked down and the spirits never scared or killed ever again.

Grace Taylor (12)

97 Holly Street

There once was a street called Holly Street. There was a lot of scary houses there. A boy called Matt knew a lot about Holly Street but most of all number 97. He once said that there was a mass murderer there. In the basement was where he killed people. No one believes this story except me, Peter Harrington.

So one day Matthew and I decided to walk down Holly Street. We saw the house. It was all boarded up. I dared Matt to go through the old rusty gates which were guarding the house, to go and look through the old letter box and count to twenty.

I said, 'And don't worry, I'll follow you.'

'I'm not scared,' he said, 'I'll do it.'

So we walked frantically through ajar gates and up the stairs to an old oak door. Matt looked in the letter box. Inside was a hallway with a couple of doors. A head poked out with a flickering candle in his hand. I felt Matt freeze.

He said, 'Ghost! There is a ghost in there!'

'Yeah, right!' I said.

So I looked in there. This was Matt's imagination. I opened the unlocked door and went in.

'Well come on Matt,' I said. I went in. I felt all the hairs on the back of my neck stand on end. In here it was freezing.

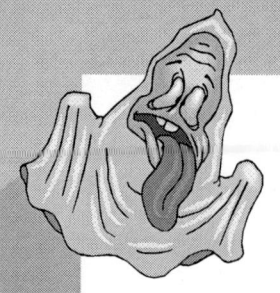

I heard the door shut behind me, so I looked back. Where was Matt? I found myself at the stairs leading to a basement. So I went down. There was an axe, a knife and a chainsaw all of which had dry, old-looking blood on them.

'Peter . . . Peter get up,' said Mum, 'or you will be late for the school bus.'

Argh, it was just a dream.

Peter Harrington (11)

The Secret Of Downs Church

Downs Church, was an old abandoned church situated in the middle of a bleak forest. Four walls, a plain stone roof and rusty metal railings surrounded it. It was a cream colour; well you could say that, from the few parts of colouration remaining on the walls. There had been a fire there, started by a group of teenagers, starved of original things to do.

No one had seen the need to go there for a long time. But the words haunted and Downs Church became associated with each other and people began to think things. A small, brown haired and pale-faced boy decided to investigate Downs Church that night.

Charles ventured on his own to the church, with his cross around his neck for comfort. He walked through the forest silently. When he caught sight of the church, he stopped.

As the foreboding fog set in, Charles slowly

opened the gate, walked to the church door, turned the handle and entered.

It was pitch-black inside, he could make out a few chairs, but that was all. He was thinking that the church felt strangely placid, when suddenly he realised he was not alone.

Out of the walls flooded black hooded monks, still troubled by the vandalism inflicted upon their church. They surrounded Charles and silently began to advance towards him.

Charles attempted to escape but was held back. As he caught a glimpse of the monks' skeletal faces, he froze dead in his tracks, fell to the ground and began to shake vigorously.

He finally escaped to live in a world of endless silence, as the fear had stolen his capability of speech.

Jamie Eve (14)

Drip, Drip, Drip

He knew that the dare was stupid. All Thomas wanted to do was prove he wasn't scared.

Thomas pushed open the door with a groan and a creak. He found he had stepped in something which seemed to be red paint. He looked up.

Drip, drip, drip.

Blood dripped slowly from a hangman's noose. A single drop of blood fell on Thomas's nose.

Drip, drip, drip.

He ran through to the next room. A terrifying chill went down his spine. He slowly swivelled around. A ghostly figure stood behind him, blood dripping from its eyes, its translucent hands reaching forward to grab Thomas's neck.

Drip, drip, drip.

Thomas scrambled into the next room. In front of him was a pale skeleton with a ghostly smile. He was wrapped in chains. Blood oozed from his bones. He moved forward but was jerked back by his chains.

From outside, Thomas's friends heard a spine-chilling yell. They looked at one another and ran inside.

They passed the hangman's noose and the ghostly figure. The hair on the back of their necks prickled. There was a deadly, spine-chilling silence.

In the next room, they heard a *drip, drip, drip*.

They looked up. There, hanging from the ceiling was Thomas. His eyes bulged out and his face was blue. Slowly, trickling down the knife in his back, a puddle of blood was forming.

It went *drip . . . drip . . . drip . . .*

Lily Kim-Sing (11)

Eyes On A Spring

There was a gate but it wasn't on its hinges. The girl stood at the gate looking at the half demolished house. Everyone said it was haunted. She had come up here to find out. She walked up the mossy path to the big, dusty, wooden door.

The door opened and the hinges creaked. She stepped into this oddly-shaped, large room cautiously.

Then all of a sudden something fell on her head. She raised her left arm. Nothing was there. There was a shadow in the centre of the room. She looked up. Somebody was up there. She shut her eyes and then opened them again. Was she daydreaming or was this thing flying straight at her?

Within seconds this black object was face to face with her. She blinked. When she reopened her eyes its bright, big yellow eyes were staring her in the face. Her pupils were fixed with her eyes wide open. Its yellow eyes were having a staring competition with her sparkling blue eyes.

Then after about a minute its eyes started turning blue, then they turned brown and at last they turned red. They stayed like that for about a minute. She blinked, its eyes got redder. Suddenly its eyes sprung out. It was like its eyes popped out on a spring but there was no spring. She screamed then froze with fright.

Suddenly a beam of light shot out of its chest and it went up in flames, leaving only its ashes behind.

Laura Stainton (11)

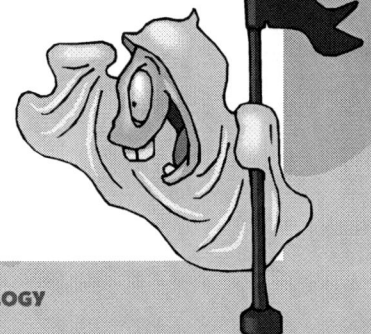

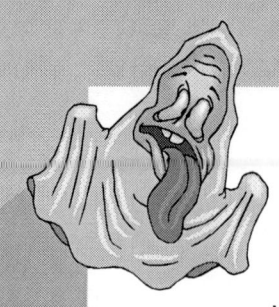

The Day Of Fear

One evening, there was a married couple and their names were Jane and James. It was Hallowe'en, and they were on their way home when suddenly they had a flat tyre.

'Oh, you wait here, Jane and I will go and find a pay phone to get a taxi home, OK? Back in a moment,' said James getting out of the car.

Jane was left alone in the car in the middle of the woods. The trees looked like grabbing hands and owls and bats screeched in the night.

Jane started to get worried, so she put the radio on and fell asleep because she was tired.

Jane woke up and found herself surrounded by lights. It was the police. A man on a loud speaker said alarmingly, 'Jane, get out of the car now!'

She was wondering if they were playing tricks on her, but they looked seriously at her.

'Jane, start walking to us and don't look behind you!'

Jane was getting really worried and wanted to know what was going on. 'What is the matter? Why can't I turn round and get back in the car?'

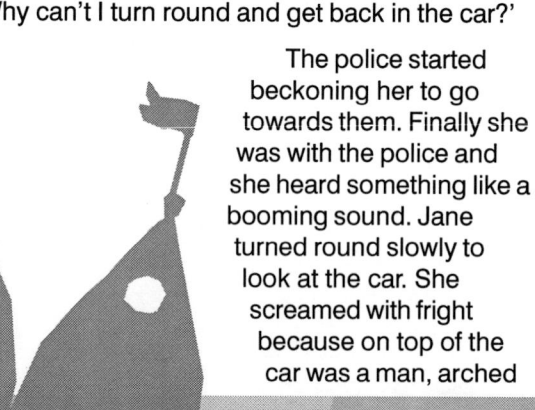

The police started beckoning her to go towards them. Finally she was with the police and she heard something like a booming sound. Jane turned round slowly to look at the car. She screamed with fright because on top of the car was a man, arched over like a gorilla with a stick in his hand with Jane's husband's head on top of it, banging it on the car. The creature's face was fierce and nasty. The creature had blood dripping from his mouth as he snarled at the police. Jane started crying and the police shouted, *'Run!'*

They ran and tried to get into the police car. The creature started to follow them. They ran over the creature and took Jane to the police station. Jane was all alone and she didn't want to go home that night, so she stayed round a policeman's house and the following morning she called her dad to come and take her home.

Once she got home, she called her sister Jenny to come and stay with her. Jane told Jenny what had happened and Jane never went to a Hallowe'en party again because she was so scared that she would see the same horrid creature again!

Rosie Ives (11)

Zombie Fright

The evening air was cold and damp. Maxine struggled to zip up her coat as she jogged towards home. She glanced at her watch, 6.30pm. The wind howled through the bare trees. The branches above her head shook and rattled like bony arms. *What a creepy night,* Maxine thought.

Glancing across the street, Maxine saw the old Gothic house looming over its creepy weed-choked lawn.

Suddenly, 'Boo!' Jenny shrieked, leaping from behind a bush.

'Jenny, you startled me.'

'Sorry, where are you off to?'

'Home,' Maxine murmured.

'Do you want to come with me to the cemetery?'

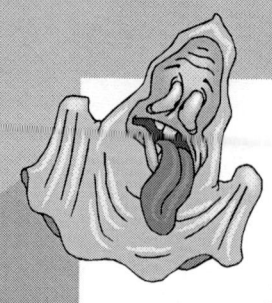

'Why would you want to go to a cemetery?'

'I'm bored, I find reading gravestones relaxing.'

Somehow Maxine was easily coerced into doing things she didn't want to but agreed. 'You're weird, yeah Mum's not home yet.'

The two girls made their way to the cemetery.

After they arrived Jenny ran deeper into the cemetery. That second, Maxine felt a splash of rain. 'Great,' she said to herself. She hurried to the mausoleum for cover. A foul odour permeated the mausoleum. She felt herself being prodded from behind.

'At last, dinner,' whispered a voice behind her.

She turned around slowly, afraid of what she might see. She screamed at the sight of a deformed zombie. Her scream seemed to echo through the hollow walls.

Maxine started to pray, hoping somehow God would hear her prayers.

'No use praying, you can't get away from me, be prepared to meet your doom.'

Suddenly the door of the mausoleum flung open. 'Maxine, are you there?' Jenny yelled from the back of the mausoleum with two burly policemen brandishing their torches behind her.

In an instant the zombie vanished into thin air leaving ashes on the floor.

'Maxine, are you alright?'

Maxine's eyes opened ever so slowly. 'Has it gone?'

'Has what gone?' Jenny replied.

'The zombie,' she replied back, her voice no more than a whisper.

'Concussion,' one of the police officer's mouthed to the other.

'Let's get her out of here,' Jenny urged.

Maxine got to her feet with the help of the policemen. As they walked out of the cemetery closing the gate behind them.

'So there's a horror story Maxine, hey you could write a story like this for your English essay,' suggested Jenny. 'It's pretty good when you think about it Maxine, you'll probably get an A for being so imaginative.'

'There's a happy story,' whispered the police to her partner as they headed to take the girls home.

What they all didn't see was the zombie's ashes swirling around on the floor only to resurrect itself.

Will history repeat itself? . . . who knows.

Senem Aysan (13)

Marbles

In the beginning there has always been marbles, as far back as I can remember, and now I sit as people all around me say I have become the very thing that I have always known and loved.

It was a bright sunny day on my sixth birthday when I was staring at Mum's old books when I was interrupted by another present put on the table. As any six-year-old would do, I was hiding under the present table when I spotted this tiny little gift with a gold ribbon wrapped around it. As curious as I was I left the tiny unknown gift until later. It wasn't until then that I realised what a wonder was hidden inside the bright gold ribbon and its neat wrapping. I left the gift until last. I was so absorbed, I forgot all about the brand new bike, the baseball and the other normal presents a six-year-old would receive. As we drew to the last present my heart was racing a mile a minute.

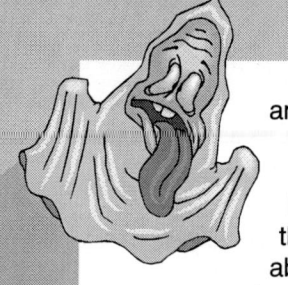

The ribbon I tore to pieces shortly followed by the wrapping paper, it was a marble, just a damned marble, I walked away in disgust. It wasn't until I was pacing around my room that I realised I had the marble tightly gripped in my hand. My life as it was known then was turned upside down, from that moment, I was no longer Alex Russell.

I became aware that when you did not desire to use this marble, it would mysteriously disappear and when you wanted to use it, you would find it within feet of where you were. Then after a while I realised that when holding the marble, I had this feeling, a bold feeling, an angry feeling, so much hate was held inside this marble.

A few weeks later after concentrating intensely, I heard the message. 'Kill Robert Winsley'. Of course I was only six and I did not even guess how much trouble this marble would bring me years later.

I could not believe what I had done in Winsley's bookstore, standing over the twenty-year-old owner, with a blood-stained knife grasped tightly in my hand. A murderer at seventeen, I covered my tracks and fled just as the sirens blared in the background of the murder scene.

It wasn't until morning that I realised what I had done. At least the cries from Master had ceased but he seemed to have a new craving, I did not want to kill any more but Master made me. My next target was a young girl, Joanne Leone, the daughter of big shot Joey Leone who owned a large section of a collection of books. It was in their company office that I killed again.

It was a cold night and I was numb all over. I knew Master would be happy when I killed her, he always is when I do as he says. She was alone in an office, room 118 I think, my palms were sweaty and I was nervous. She turned to face me and well, I froze, as if surprised to see a smiling face staring back at me. I thought to myself, *I'm a monster now* . . . I killed her, chopped her up into little bits and cried, tears running down my cheeks, I'm a monster. Again and again I see her smiling face staring back at me. How, how could I have killed again? I'll never forgive myself.

I got home later that evening and cried myself to sleep, despite me being distraught, Master was happy. I didn't know who it was but it had possessed me and it wanted more. The marble glowed white when messages were sent between us. I kept trying to ask who or what it was but no answer would come. The only message it was sending me was where and when I would kill again. I was going home.

Everything seemed familiar inside the old living room, my room, it was great apart from the rotting body of my mother. I could have sworn I was in Heaven. The strange thing was I enjoyed killing my mother and now I was a full time serial killer.

Eventually I was caught, a bit too late for the families of thirty-eight dead book collectors around the country. You know this is the first time I've ever told anyone my story, a pity the mysterious marble was never caught but here I am with a death sentence. Then again maybe I

A YOUNG WRITERS ANTHOLOGY

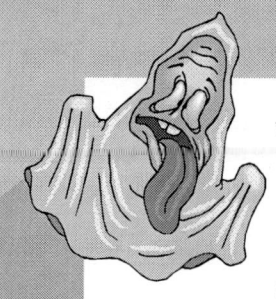

wasn't controlled by an anonymous madman, maybe I just lost my marbles.

Josh Logan (12)

Cannibal Parents

Once there were two parents who spoilt their daughter Persephone absolutely rotten. You name it she had it.

One night there was a movie on the box that Persephone wanted to watch. Her parents said no because Persephone was too young. Persephone pleaded, she almost cried, but her parents would not crack. Persephone steamed upstairs, pulled out her pet spiders and then threw them on her mother and father and ran back upstairs again. Persephone lay listening to her parents scream much to her delight.

At 11 o'clock Persephone woke to a growling sound downstairs, she ignored it and started to doze. Five minutes later she woke again to heavy footsteps climbing the stairs. She was petrified. The footsteps ended, no noise from downstairs. What was happening?

Suddenly the door creaked open and there stood the silhouettes of her parents. Persephone tried to apologise but her father pounced and kicked her in the head, which killed her instantly.

Persephone's mother started to nibble her dead daughter's hand, then her arm and then her neck, but before she reached the head Persephone's father joined in and ate the head whole.

They together feasted on their daughter's carcass until her bones were licked clean. After

Persephone's parents' meal, they hid Persephone's bones under her wardrobe.

Next day the police were searching the house for an odour that was smelt by the next-door neighbour. The police found Persephone's body under the wardrobe and buried her. As for her parents they're still out there . . .

Hannah Redman (12)

Saturday Night At The Graveyard

It was 8 o'clock on a Saturday night. Billy was visiting his grandad's grave. As Billy walked he saw cobwebs. He heard bats, owls, rustling of leaves. It was dark, cold, wet and grey. Billy was getting scared.

As Billy walked dead people were coming out of their graves and following Billy. Billy started to jog, he got faster. As he ran the skeletons ran. The skeletons surrounded him.

'How dare you run over our graves.'

'Look what they've done to me,' the skeletons were saying spookily.

Billy ran to the church. As he entered the church the gate closed. He turned around and saw skeletons with their hands out of the bars trying to get him. A dead dog came out and bit Billy's leg. Billy jumped back, the skeleton grabbed him.

Billy found a gate, he tried to open it but he was too tired. 'Help!' Billy screamed. Billy was very scared.

'All I came to do was visit my grandad,' Billy shouted.

The arms were still coming out of the bars.

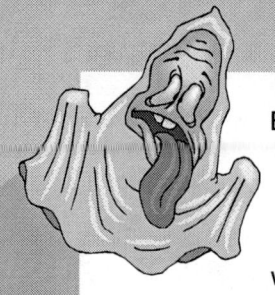

Billy turned around, in one of the cells the skeletons were breaking through the bars.

All the skeletons had broken through.

After ten minutes a skeleton stepped forward and said, 'Right let's settle this over a pack of cards, you win you go but if I win you're dead.'

Billy sat down sheepishly, the skeleton dealt the cards. They played poker. Billy lost.

'Off with his head!' the skeletons chanted.

The skeleton chopped off Billy's head. Billy was dead.

Catherine Smith (12)

A Ghastly Tale Of Ghoulish Terror

It was dark, pitch-black, infinite nothingness. Only the ominous hooting of a solitary owl shattered the unearthly silence. The house stood isolated on the hill, looking innocent enough to the unwitting passer-by and from the exterior revealed little of the fiendish events that happened in the dead of night. As the church bells chime for the witching hour, the house comes alive. The floorboards groan with anticipation and . . .

Wait!

This is all so predictable! So here is a tale of mischief, a saga of intrigue but there is no deserted house with numerous meandering corridors, windowpanes that rattle menacingly in the zephyr or lifeless abodes where the only movement is rising damp.

Replace the smell of medieval rotting beams with that of a newly varnished wooden floor, the monotonous ticking of a grandfather clock with the occasional beeping of an electronic scoreboard. For this ghoulish fable will reveal that the seemingly harmless school gym conceals secrets more hideous than the contents of your PE bag. So if you thought the sight of your games teacher in a gym skirt was frightening enough, think again.

The pupils of yesteryear still inhabit the gym (in spirit anyway) to make sure you have to brave the elements like they had to. They hide the keys when the weather is inclement so the doors remain locked and you are forced outside. Why should you be able to play in a dry, heated sports hall when they couldn't? So the next time your hands are freezing in the blistering cold, remember that spirits are at work and the seemingly vacant gym is not all it appears.

Ruth Morris (17)

Hallucinations

The doctor entered the silent room, to see his new client in the corner of it. She was clutching her legs in fear, tears streaming down her cheeks and two round eyes paralysed in the state of fear. He could hear her breathing heavily. He kneeled down beside her. Placing his hand on her shoulder as a sign of comfort.

'Lola?' asked the doctor.

She nodded.

'Again was it?'

He was talking about those absurd hallucinations she had of ghosts, predicting future horrific events.

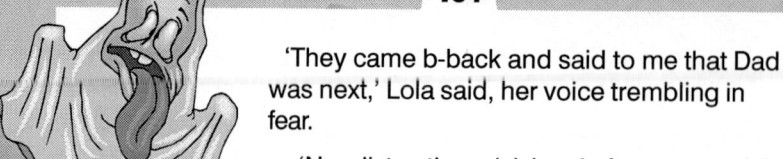

'They came b-back and said to me that Dad was next,' Lola said, her voice trembling in fear.

'Now listen these 'visions' of yours are tricks of the mind, your mum's waiting outside, I will ask her to take you home. I will carry out some research on these 'visions'.'

The doctor called her mother in who was pacing up and down the corridor in anticipation. As soon as she saw her daughter she let out a squeal of joy, and gave her a hug, and also giving a very meaningful stare. They went to the car, which reflected the midnight-blue sky and went home in serenity.

They arrived to their house. Lola still slightly shocked from her latest 'vision'. They opened the front door to find large dollops of sunset-red blood circling the lifeless body of Lola's father. Every inch of him stabbed. Lola edged towards him and collapsed at the familiar sight.

Nina Klair (14)

My Ghost Story

Coming back from Tamara's. Home alone. The electricity's gone, I'm just going to use a candle and go to the kitchen to get some matches. The window's nets are flapping. The cutlery jingles. *'Argh!'* Something brushes past my leg and scratches it. I stagger towards the top drawer to get the matches but I find the torch and I use that instead. I switch it on and shine it onto the creature, which to my relief is only my cat.

I tiptoe up the stairs, creep across the landing and turn my door handle only to find it's locked. It's the bathroom door . . . Hang on a minute, the door can only be locked from the inside. I sprint into the opposite direction, jump into my room, shut the door and lock it. I sit. Listen. I hear breathing outside my door. I hear a scream. Then I hear a voice.

It's whispering, 'Let me in.'

I unlock my door to find my brother covered in blood. He falls into my arms, squashing me. He squirts tomato sauce into my face. The electric comes back on. I shove my brother out of my room and watch my telly.

Oh no, the electric's gone again. *'Argh!'*

Carrieann Machin (11)

Pomponi Does Poe

In the dark I heard a strange noise, I left my room and had a look around. I heard gentle knocking at the door, just a quiet tapping at my door. 'Who's there?' I called, as the tapping sped up. No answer only knocking, knocking at my door. I walked towards the door and picked up an umbrella. 'I'm armed, show yourself,' I called out.

Again no answer, only tapping. That annoying gentle knocking at the door. I reached to the door knob and slowly turned it. The door swung open but nothing in sight.

I closed the door behind me, but the tapping carried on. That irritating little tapping on my door, the creature gave a cough. I thought to myself, *why is this thing coughing?* Coughing and knocking at my door. I pulled back the curtain and took a glance. I saw a shadow, but I could make it out. If there is a shadow, there must be a body.

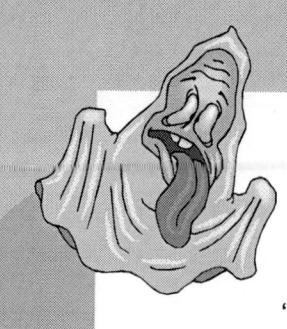

I walked out of my house and followed the shadow to where it was coming from, then I saw it . . . the shadow was an in-human being, a strange creature that was wearing a cape.

'Who are you?' I asked.

He didn't answer but I saw a tear run down his cheek.

'Why are you crying?' I asked him.

Again he didn't reply, he just flew into the night sky.

'Wait!' I called out to him, but he never returned.

The mystery still remains; he visited me and no one else.

Yasmin Pomponi (13)

The Haunted Mansion

'Argh!' came a scream from the mansion.

I had to find out what was making it. Rumours had it that the place was haunted, or was it? Maybe it was the neighbour's spoilt brat having his weekly scream, I don't know what it was, I've heard that the first night the owners slept there they were found dead the next morning.

I couldn't concentrate at school at all.

'Faiza, stop daydreaming and concentrate on your work,' my teacher shouted.

Everyone was staring at me, I was totally embarrassed. My cheeks looked as red as a cherry, I tried to concentrate the whole day.

When school was over I decided that I should investigate the haunted mansion. I had spare time so I thought it would be a good idea, luckily I had my torch with me so if things got frightening I could use it. I took ten minutes to get there but finally I had made it.

I was standing in front of the haunted mansion, it was grey and gloomy, as if the life was sucked right out of it. I was terrified but determined to find out what or who had made the screams.

I stepped in the first room . . .

It was the dining room because it had sofas and a table with chairs surrounding it. Suddenly I heard the scream, it was coming from the corridor. I dashed as fast as a cheetah. In front of me I saw two ghosts, you could tell they were ghosts because you could see right through them.

I had finally solved the mystery, it was a ghost having its usual weekly hair cut!

Faiza Hussain (12)

Should Have Said No!

It was a dark December night and Sarah was getting ready to go to Emma's house. There was knock at the door.

'Come in,' shouted Sarah.

'Hello, would you like a lift to Emma's?'

'Yes, thanks Mum.'

Sarah got excited. Her mum called her. They set off. Emma was waiting outside.

'Hiya Emma.'

'Hiya mate,' said Emma.

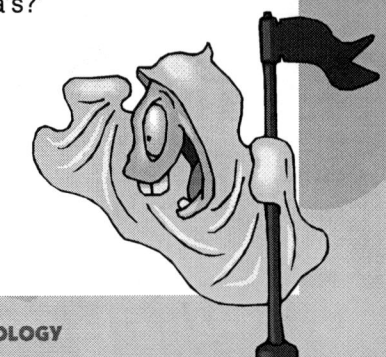

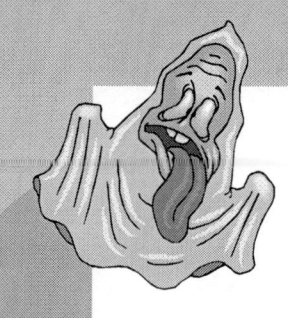

'See you at 10pm, Mum.'

'OK.'

'Oh, has Mummy got to pick you up 'cause it will be dark?' said Emma sarcastically.

'I won't walk because of the dark.'

'Why are you so scared?'

'OK then.' Sarah shouted, '*Mum*, I'm walking.'

'It will be dark.'

'I'm walking, OK.'

Sarah walked into Emma's house as her mum drove off in worry.

Two hours later Sarah looked at her watch, it was 9.55pm. 'I must start walking home now.'

'OK.'

She set off. Her feet crunching in the snow. The famous haunted house was near, she was scared but desperate to look inside. She stepped in. A bony hand waved in her face. She screamed. She tried to get out but fell down a hole. The hand followed. There was an open window.

She got home, no lights were on. She went to the kitchen, flicked the light switch on. Nothing came on. She tried to sit at the table but couldn't. She sat at the other side. She could hear tapping low and far away. It got louder and nearer. Her hands were shaking. She felt breathing down her neck. Hard and loud.

Sarah Tapsell (13)

The Bedroom Ghost

When a friend of mine moved into a new house she couldn't go to sleep. At the time she was three years old. Her mum and dad would put her to bed, but about five minutes later she would get up and start to play with her toys.

Her parents asked why she didn't want to go to sleep. She told them that the little girl was waking her up and wanted to play. My friend didn't have any brothers or sisters so her parents were really confused.

They asked, 'What little girl?'

She pointed at the radiator and said, 'That little girl.'

Her parents got really scared and didn't know what to think so they let her sleep in their room.

First her parents went to see the neighbours and asked if they knew about the little girl. They didn't. Then her dad went to see a woman that knew things about ghosts and told her the story. The woman told her dad to put her in her room that night and wait for her to go to sleep, then go downstairs and wait for the ghost to wake her up and when the ghost did wake her up to go upstairs and shout at the ghost.

'Tell it to go away and leave her alone.'

That night her dad shouted at the ghost. After that she slept all through the night with no problems.

Moa Karlin Josefsson (9)

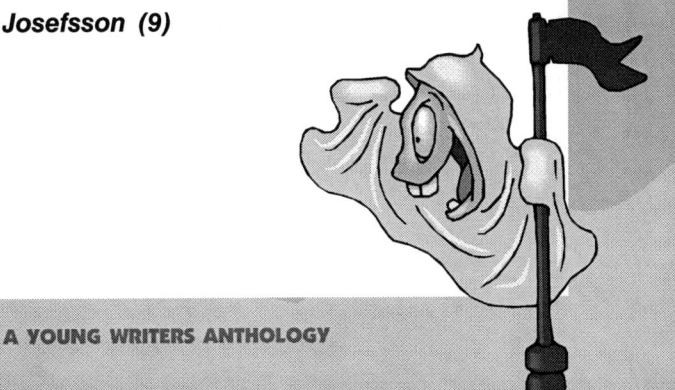

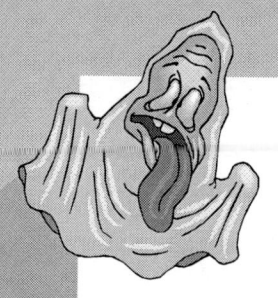

Ghost House

Paige, Amy and their friend, Luke, decided to explore an old house that looked empty.

Paige got there first. She opened the door and slowly went up the creaky, dusty stairs. The door slammed shut behind her. Paige stood still. She heard, 'Whoooo'. It sounded ghostly but there was nobody around. Paige shouted, 'Amy, Amy, Amy!'

Amy was banging at the door. Eventually she got it open. 'Don't go in there alone,' Amy said. 'My mam says ghosts and a strange old lady live here.'

Two days later, Paige, Amy and Luke returned. They were curious and wanted to know more. They politely knocked this time. An old lady opened the door. She asked them to come in. She said that there were no ghosts in the house. Paige did not believe her.

The children decided to come back at night. They went into the house through a cellar door. It was dark, cold and creepy. They overheard the old lady arguing with somebody but there was nobody there but a fine blue mist. It turned yellow and the children watched as it wrapped itself round the old lady and strangled her. The children jumped out of their hiding place to save her but it was too late. She'd stopped breathing.

All this happened 66 years ago. Paige is an old lady herself now and she sometimes tells her grandchildren the story of the old lady and her ghostly end.

Paige Burnham (8)

Winter Woods

One cold winter evening when Chenel Adams was walking home after a night clubbing with her wild, outrageous friends, she heard strange and bizarre noises. Of course she thought she was hearing things, so she carried on down the path, but no, she wasn't hearing things. It started to snow. She only had a thin jacket on. She was now getting cold.

Chenel was now frightened and walking faster than ever. The trees were blowing hard and branches were hitting Chenel's face. She started to run, faster and faster. She looked behind every minute; her shoes were hurting the soles of her feet.

'Yoo-who, yoo-who!' yelled a white floating object which was transparent.

'Argh!' screamed Chenel as she ran back the other way, her heart beating faster than ever. She tried to catch up with her friends. She couldn't see any of them. She came out of the woods. She looked behind her, nothing.

'Yoo-who, yoo-who!' screamed the ghost again.

She ran into the road. A hippy car came down the street, it was travelling so fast that it couldn't stop. She went over the top of the car.

She woke up in hospital. She couldn't move her arm.

'Hello, how are you?' yelled the ghost again. 'Yoo-who, yoo-who, helloooo!' the ghost shrieked.

'Leave me alone, leave me alone!' shouted Chenel.

'Why, don't you want me here?' asked the ghost.

'No, I don't, get out, get out!' bellowed Chenel again.

A YOUNG WRITERS ANTHOLOGY

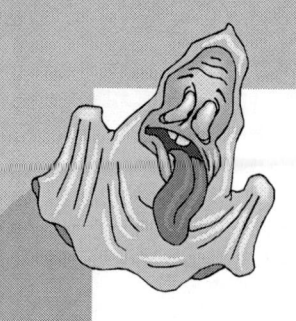

'No, I'm going to stay with you forever. Ha, ha, ha, ha!' said the ghost with joy.

'Noooooooo!' yelled Chenel.

Jennifer Langton-Goh (11)
Manning Comprehensive School, Nottingham

The Canal's Secret

It had been six days since Harley disappeared. The police said that they should find the body easily in nine days if it was in the catchment area.

'Well, nobody knows what happened that Friday night,' reported a neighbour. 'I saw her walk down the road and turn the corner to her friend's house. I didn't watch her anymore walking down the street because I didn't think I needed to so I drew the curtains and went to sleep'.

Well, what happened to Harley we're about to find out.

She walked to her friend's house; it was misty and dark on that night. These were her last thoughts, *it's cold tonight, who's that, oh no it's him, he's coming closer. Argh, get off me.* That was the last she ever knew.

This is the police report about Harley when they found the body.

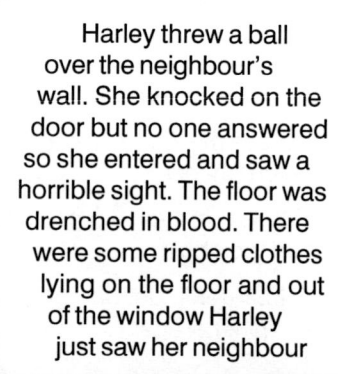

Harley threw a ball over the neighbour's wall. She knocked on the door but no one answered so she entered and saw a horrible sight. The floor was drenched in blood. There were some ripped clothes lying on the floor and out of the window Harley just saw her neighbour throw his wife in the canal through his garden. The neighbour caught Harley's eye and then decided that he would murder her so that she couldn't tell anyone his secret, and that's what happened. The strange thing is that Harley's body was found with the neighbour's wife in exactly the same place.

Alice Logan (12)
Manning Comprehensive School, Nottingham

Ghostly Melissa

The wind was howling. The trees were alive; there was some rustling in the wind. Melissa was picking up firewood...

She looked around. No one was around, nothing and no one knew what she was doing.

'Whoooo!'

There was a noise. Melissa turned round suddenly. She was thinking to herself that she was a poor girl in this horror movie. As she began to pick up some more firewood, the noise was getting louder, nearer and scarier. Melissa didn't realise this because she was trying to block out all the scary noises.

Melissa finished picking up the firewood then she turned around . . .

'Roar!'

Melissa jumped with fright. She saw a tall figure. It was wearing a long black cloak. The hooded figure was stepping closer and closer to Melissa. She didn't move because she was paralysed with fright.

The figure took off its hood and whispered in her ear, 'Invisible toads!'

Melissa was so scared that she ran home.

The figure faded away in the moonlight. Melissa was so scared she tripped. She stumbled upon a lake full of bright colours. She suddenly felt secure.

Melissa sat by the lake, all of the terrifying noises around her stopped and she began to hum and sing, but only quietly because she didn't want the hooded figure to come back. She was hot and exhausted so she scooped some water and poured it over her beautiful face. Melissa looked into the lake. She saw nothing. Melissa screamed . . .

Chenel Poyzer (12)
Manning Comprehensive School, Nottingham

The Haunted Basement

Rumours were spread that there was a thing named 'The Haunted Basement'. Was it the truth or was it a lie? I know that this is the truth and it wasn't long until someone had known of it as well.

Long, long ago this story was told and from that day onwards people wouldn't let their children go out because someone would be lurking, waiting so they could *strike* and then they could lock the child in the basement and throw away the key. It's terrible and if it ever happens to you, take my word for it, *scream!* You do not want to be in this position and if you were, don't even think about crying to mummy because it will be too late. If you want to step out of that door it better be for a good reason.

Maybe that you think

that you won't bother because you've got your gang and they will sort them out, but they won't because even though you have 100 people, the mysterious lurking people have more so I have warned you, stay out of their way.

I've had experience and that experience is not good. It happened once. The person was . . . *me!*

Sidra Jamil (11)
Manning Comprehensive School, Nottingham

Brother

I was running, but my legs didn't move. I was screaming, but there was no sound and it was coming closer. Suddenly I tripped. When I got up I was on Alamo Beach.

The day was misty and the tide was starting to come in. As I walked along the beach I could see an old house upon a sand dune. I thought it was a bit strange as I had never seen it before, but I just thought, *oh well,* and decided to go and explore.

As the door creaked open I could see something scurrying across the floor. As it scurried into the pale light I was frozen on the spot. It was a sheep-like creature and it smelt of rotting flesh and its eyes were just black holes and its scream made my ears bleed. Suddenly I heard a scream and realised it was coming for me and my legs were finally moving.

As the hot, gooey blood ran down my face, I had run up at least seven flights of stairs and ended up in a large room, which I assumed was the attic.

Suddenly I heard a very wispy voice say, 'It wasn't my fault you fell. But you wouldn't believe me, and now look at me.' He began to come towards me. 'How could you do this to your own brother?'

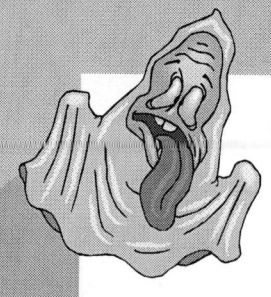

'I'm sorry, I didn't know.'

'No, you wouldn't would you, but now you're going to pay.'

I felt something bite my neck. I quickly thrust it off, ran towards the window and jumped out of it.

Tammy Sills (12)
Manning Comprehensive School, Nottingham

Horror House

Boom! Bash! Bang! Crash! I heard as I walked into the kitchen. I looked in the room to see that it was completely bare until I looked up and there were all the ghosts juggling the cooker.

The ghosts looked a bit on the odd side. They had these odd black holes for their eyes, lips and nose. Now I know what you think I am going to put next, you think I am going to say that they looked like white sheets, but I am not. They looked like ordinary people but with those weird faces and of course they could fly.

Their clothes were all ripped and torn and looked like they had been rolling all over in the mud and stamped on.

They started to fly down towards me. I thought that was it, I thought I was going to die, but then they started to sing to me and they were being dead nice to me, ha, ha, ha, do you get it when I say *dead* nice to me?

Anyway, I started to sing along with them and we were having a really good time until I wanted to go home. I tried to open the door but it was locked.

All the ghosts turned on me and said, 'You are doomed to stay in here for the rest of you life!'

Amy Donnelly (12)
Manning Comprehensive School, Nottingham

More Than Just A Trip

The coach screeched to a halt. We stared out of the window at the dismal building before us. The hotel was a narrow grey building plonked in the middle of a noisy traffic-filled road.

Trisha grimaced. 'Oh great, I bet they've got mice as well.'

Trish and I moaned as we dragged our luggage up the steps. A cranky wrinkled old bat introduced herself as Mrs Fresh. She didn't smell fresh. We were all led to our rooms; Trisha and I were placed in a dusty room on the top floor next to the caretaker's closet. We weren't impressed.

That night we both had terrible nightmares. This happened for the following nights until we decided to stay awake so we didn't dream. The clock struck twelve and I saw Trisha had fallen asleep. I was wondering whether to wake her or not when suddenly her eyes opened wide and she leapt from her chair onto me. I opened my mouth but no sound came out. I clawed at the floor trying to stop her in the process of dragging me towards the door, but Trisha had suddenly gained a new strength and soon I was flung into the caretaker's closet. As the door closed on us I saw that this was no closet. I slowly turned my gaze towards the man before me.

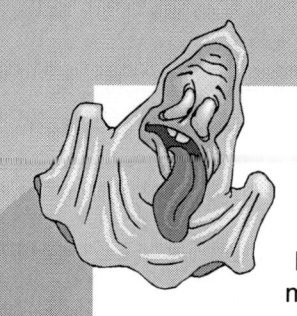

He held an axe above me and was about to swoop down and behead me when, on impulse, I grabbed his legs, I reached for the door handle, *I'm gonna make it,* but I was betting without Trisha, as suddenly she pulled me down on the ground. I was dead.

Jessica Shilton (12)
Manning Comprehensive School, Nottingham

The Abandoned Forest

Kate, a seven-year-old girl, was walking through an abandoned forest which no one would have dared entered. She only had a little confidence in herself. Half of her heart told her to carry on, but the other half didn't. She didn't know what to do. In the end she decided to carry on. She kept on having weird thoughts. She began walking slowly but suddenly froze after seeing a dead skeleton hanging in front of her.

'Argh!' Kate screamed louder than ever. She tried running as fast as she could, her heart kept on thumping really fast. She noticed a white blurry thing (not knowing it was a ghost). She kept her eye out for anyone behind her.

Just then her eye caught on an unusual thing lying asleep on the ground beside her foot. It had a long body, half of it was a dog's body and the other half was a human's head. It was lying down as if it was dead. She reached out, her arms shaking of fear. The unusual thing jumped up and bit off Kate's hand. Kate went blank, she didn't even let out a squeak. She fainted beside the dog.

When she woke up she found herself in hospital. 'Why am I here? I'm not ill,' she muttered to herself in an unusual way. She lifted her hand to rub her eyes when 'Argh!' she screamed out so loud that all the nurses came rushing in.

Adeeka Najabat (11)
Manning Comprehensive School, Nottingham

The Ghost Of Emily

On a street, there stood an old house that was no longer being used. Every villager that passed by would walk by it as fast as they could. Weird things happened when they went into the house. It seemed that history repeated itself.

A long time ago, a family came and stayed at the house. Their daughter, Emily, was really kind. But there was something about her that was so secretive that nobody knew. One day, when Emily's friend asked her about her family, she refused to answer and that made her friend curious about her.

A few months later, there was a story telling competition in Emily's school. When the results were announced, Emily had won the first place. Her story had been read by the teacher and the class was amazed by it, but in the middle of the story, Emily screamed and ran from class. She was nowhere in sight the week after. Nobody knew where she was, including her best friend Katie.

A few days after, Katie went to Emily's house. She knocked on the door but there was no answer. Suddenly the door opened. In the hope of talking to Emily, Katie went in. The first thing that she saw was the bodies of Emily's parents. Too late, they were all dead. By the look on their faces, they looked shocked. Katie searched for Emily hoping that she was still alive.

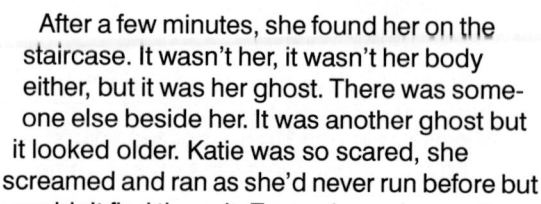

After a few minutes, she found her on the staircase. It wasn't her, it wasn't her body either, but it was her ghost. There was someone else beside her. It was another ghost but it looked older. Katie was so scared, she screamed and ran as she'd never run before but she couldn't find the exit. Everywhere she ran the ghost seemed to follow her. She ran until she was back in the hallway but it was too late. The ghosts were there and they were approaching her really fast until they were completely covering her.

Days went by but Katie never came out. People who tried to find her in Emily's house all ended up the same. Many people kept going missing until they stopped searching when they'd read Emily's story. The story's about a girl that was being followed by her grandfather's ghost and when she died, she became a ghost. That's what happened to Emily. The reason she screamed and ran out of class was because she couldn't take it, so she ran home and killed herself. That's what truly happened to Emily. A tragic ending of a girl.

Syabilla Wan Saadan (13)
Manning Comprehensive School, Nottingham

The Big Mistake

As we walked through what seemed like a deserted passage leading to the hushed graveyard, there was a feeling of major tension in the cold air. Though we did not know what it was, all three of us were positive that there was something lurking behind us . . . something strange . . .

something not right. This made us all feel uneasy and anxious.

The cold air pressed against our troubled faces as we strolled through the neglected path, which was concealed with over-run dreary grass and with bunches of wilted flowers here and there. Every step we took, the thought of hope was dying. We neared to the foot of the graveyard; a combination of both fear and anxiety entered our minds, not knowing whether to proceed or to turn back. Our anxiety got the better of us, so we quickened our pace as we were determined to achieve our goal.

The gate separating the path and the graveyard was covered with crispy, decaying ivy which clung to the rusty iron bars of the gate. We had now entered the graveyard, which was towered by overgrown shrubbery and lofty trees, which swayed from side to side creating a feeling of eeriness. As we tiptoed at a snail's pace, to the centre of the graveyard, puzzled question entered our minds . . . *Why did we have to play near a graveyard? Why did we ever think of playing hide-and-seek? Why did Liam wander off? Were we ever going to find him? Was he still alive?* We started searching for him. We looked everywhere; behind the trees, behind the graves, we even started calling his name, but there was no sign of him.

In the far distance we heard weak wailing and screaming. It seemed as if someone or something was in danger . . . in pain. We headed towards the troubled noises but suddenly the wailing stopped. The three of us exchanged glances, full of terror. At that precise moment something clutched my exhausted shoulder. I gasped. My heart began to beat faster than ever. My cold fingers felt numb and insensitive. My body felt as if it was full of ice and that icy water was flowing through my body, but somehow I gathered my courage and turned around. It was Liam. For a complete minute, not even one of us uttered a sound. We were awestruck. If felt as if our mouths had no strength left to even speak. We then realised that there was something different about Liam.

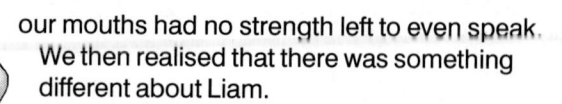

He looked pale and had blood trickling down his left ear and silent tears pouring down his weary cheeks. His pain was unbearable, so I reached out to help him but just then he collapsed to the ground with a heavy thud. We were all dumbstruck. We didn't know what to do. All I could think of was to run for help. As I got up to get help, once again continuous wailing filled the air, but it couldn't have been Liam, so who was it? What was out there?

Asma Hussain (12)
Manning Comprehensive School, Nottingham

One Ghostly Day

One grey and ghostly day it was very cold. There was a little girl called Gemma who lived near the woods. She had to go to the shop for her mum. Gemma was lonely and scared. She was only 13 years of age.

She was walking through the woods on her own to get home. As she went through the woods it got darker and darker. It got very late and a noise appeared from owls, wolves and loads more animals. Gemma got more and more scared as she went along. When Gemma got to the end she saw her mum, Alison, and her dad, Stacy. Gemma was so pleased to see them that she ran as fast as she could to them.

Gemma got sent to bed after dinner, but she

couldn't get to sleep with all the spooky noises.

She got up the next morning and saw her mum on the floor with her dad sitting beside her. Gemma asked what was wrong.

Her dad said, 'Somebody was at the door last night and that person shot her.'

Gemma ran upstairs crying and flung herself on the bed. She thought, *who's next to be killed? Will it be me, or will I be left on my own and my dad be killed instead? Will my mum come and haunt me and my dad?*

Her dad went upstairs to see if she was alright.

'Will you come and choose what to put on your mum Gemma?' he asked.

Melissa Martin (11)
Manning Comprehensive School, Nottingham

The Haunted Mansion

It as the night before Hallowe'en and the Jones family decided to take a vacation to somewhere other than Skegness. The two brats, John and Sarah, were extremely foolish and wanted to go to the haunted resort mansion. It was said, 200 years ago a young woman was murdered there and she will haunt the mansion till she receives her revenge.

John and Sarah were waiting in the car, while Mother and Father were checking in. An hour later their parents were not back and the two children were very worried.

'John, Mother and Father are not back and we are here in this dark, cold forest alone, if you have not noticed. What shall we do? Aren't you scared?'

John tried looking tough, holding in his

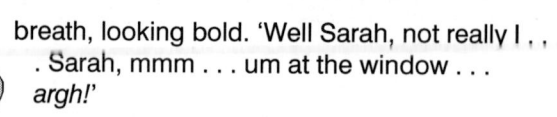

breath, looking bold. 'Well Sarah, not really I . . . Sarah, mmm . . . um at the window . . . argh!'

Standing a few inches away from the window was Mrs Jones with no skin, no lips, no clothes. She was scraping at the window screaming so loudly you could not hear the thunder! The two children were screaming, and sweat dripped off their faces.

Sarah tried to undo the opposite door to escape, but as she and John climbed out, his shoe lace got caught in a tree root which had come alive to stop him from running!

'Sarah help me!'

Sarah was too scared to run back so she kept on running, hearing her brother's screams.

Twenty years later, the screams still haunt her and she lives in fear, knowing she was the next Jones family member victim.

Jade McQueen (12)
Manning Comprehensive School, Nottingham

The Mystery Glow

It was a dark and dull afternoon. I was walking my dog in the local park. I saw a light coming from behind a bush. My dog started to bark, what was this all about? I went to investigate.

As I got closer to the glow it ceased and everything went back to normal, so I ran home and told my mum all about it.

The next day I went back to the park, it happened again so I quickly ran to where the glow was and it kept glowing.

I soon found out that it wasn't a light bulb it was a horseshoe! When I touched it the wind blew my face and it started to thunder and rain. Everyone ran to find cover but I just stood there dumbstruck.

So I took it home and showed my mum. She wouldn't believe me when I told her so I went to bed, very tired.

I had an amazing dream; a spirit told me that the horseshoe was cursed.

These were its exact words: 'Do not show anyone else the horseshoe, because if you do you will be cursed for the rest of your life!'

It was next morning and still shaken from my weird dream, I went downstairs to have breakfast. I decided not to tell anyone about my dream because they might think I was mad.

I wasn't sure whether the spirit was telling the truth or not but I still showed my friends the horseshoe and now every time I see a horseshoe I wonder if it is magic. I still don't know if I am cursed or not.

Melike Louise Berker (11)
Manning Comprehensive School, Nottingham

The Nightmare

'It's time to go to bed,' my mum shouted.

I got my school things ready for the next day and went straight to bed. I couldn't wait for tomorrow, my friends and me are going on a trip to a museum.

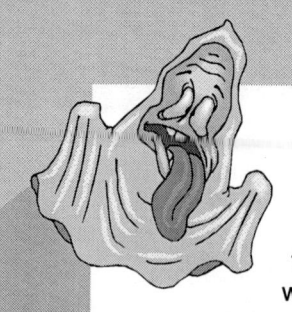

After a while I went to sleep and these scary things came to me in my dream about tomorrow's trip. It was my friends and me, we were looking at pictures and were very happy, but then we saw a picture, it was something that we had never seen before, it had red eyes.

Then my friends and me were running from that thing - from that picture - it looked like a ghost. Then the ghost started to fly faster and faster. We started to get even more scared, we didn't know what to do. Then the ghost grabbed me and started to squeeze me and my ribs started to crack together.

Then I screamed so loud that my mum came to my room and asked me what happened. I told her about my dream.

She said, 'Don't worry love it was only dream.'

The next day I went to school and told all my friends what had happened in my dream and they started to laugh. Then we went to our trip and had a wonderful time without that ghost, and we really did see a picture just like that ghost in my dream. Scary or what?

Aram Mahfooz (13)
Manning Comprehensive School, Nottingham

A YOUNG WRITERS ANTHOLOGY

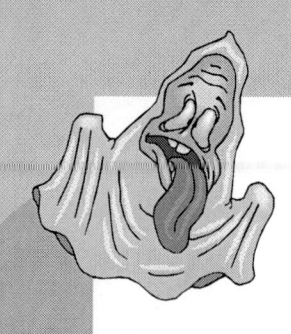

Information

We hope you have enjoyed reading this book - and that you will continue to enjoy it in the coming years.

If you like reading and writing drop us a line, or give us a call, and we'll send you a free information pack.

Write to:
Young Writers Information, Remus House, Coltsfoot Drive, Woodston, Peterborough PE2 9JX Tel: 01733 890066 or check out our website at www.youngwriters.co.uk.